D1500550

BEACHFRONT PROMISES

SOLOMONS ISLAND SERIES BOOK TWO

MICHELE GILCREST

CHAPTER 1

*C*lara finished restocking the stationary in the back room and descended from the stepladder to prep for the end of the day. The digital alarm sounded on her watch, signaling that it was almost four o'clock. She contemplated if tonight's menu options would include baked ziti, one of the Wednesday night specials at the café, or if she'd pick up something to grill outdoors on this beautiful summer evening.

"Hey, gorgeous," Mike said as he peeked inside the stockroom.

"Mike, you startled me. What are you doing back here?" Clara asked.

"Just checking on you, that's all."

"Ha, tell the truth. That's never all with you.

There's a hidden agenda in there somewhere," she said.

Mike entered the room and closed the door behind him. He removed the step ladder from Clara's hands and put it away before turning to sneak in a sweet kiss.

"You're right. I have a hidden agenda. It's stealing all the kisses I can before I head out on the evening tour with Tommy," he responded.

"You are so bad. One of these days we're going to push our luck and get caught."

"Why are we still sneaking around, anyway?" he asked.

Mike drew Clara in by the waist and kissed her again before trying to plead his case.

After a gentle touch on the cheeks, he spoke in a low voice.

"If you think about it, I'll primarily be working at the new location in the next thirty days. We're just waiting for the crew to finish up the last few touches with the renovations. Our new hire, Tommy, is almost done with his training, and he's just about ready to take over my shifts here. Is it really necessary that we continue to keep our feelings a secret?" he asked.

"Mike, you know it makes me feel terrible when you put it like that. I don't want to keep anything a secret. I'm just trying to do things the right way and maintain some sort of dignity here. Think about it. In everyone else's eyes, I'm the assistant who's only been working here for, what? Maybe four months? I just want to do this right. Trust me, it has nothing to do with me not wanting to be with you," she said, speaking the truth.

"I know, but you are aware that everyone here adores you, right? Besides, Ms. Mae is no fool. She already suspects something is up between us, and the guys... well, they would never comment to begin with," he said in a somber voice.

"I know, but still. Just hang in there a little while longer, for me. Thirty days isn't that far away."

"Then, after that, I get to profess my feelings for you to the entire world?"

"Yes, to the entire wide world, I promise. I just don't like the stigma that goes along with the assistant having a rendezvous with her boss. You've been nothing but the perfect gentleman, but you can understand that, can't you?" Clara asked.

"Yes, I get it."

"Good, so do we have a deal? We're going to wait at least a month until you start working out of the new location?" she said while tugging on his shirt.

"We have a deal, but in order to make it official, let's seal it with one more kiss."

She indulged him for a few heated moments before clearing her throat, straightening out her clothing, and telling him to scoot.

"Hey, Mike," she whispered.

"Yeah?"

"Wipe the lipstick off your face before you go."

He checked a mirror nearby and freshened up.

"Ms. Clara Covington, I cannot wait to do right by you. Soon, we're going to walk hand in hand so that all of Solomons Island knows how much I care for you. You just wait. In thirty days... you'll see."

She giggled and straightened out his collar for him.

"I know you will. Now get out there and enjoy your boat tour with Tommy."

He pecked her on the forehead and ducked back into the hallway just as quickly as he slipped in.

～

Clara's longtime friend, Mackenzie, was working the evening shift across the street at the café. She was settling in her new role as manager and had a knack for drawing in the locals to eat and bond over card games, sewing clubs, and even sports. This evening would be no exception. The members of the Wednesday bridge club were filing in, rearranging tables to eat and prep for their first round of bridge.

"Josh. How's it going?" Clara asked, making herself comfortable in her favorite seat.

"Oh, you know, it's going. It's bridge night, and Mackenzie is running around like a chicken with her head cut off trying to accommodate Mrs. Dudley, who prefers the Monday night special instead of tonight's special. Mackenzie is much more patient than I am. It's becoming such a regular habit. I would just tell the woman she needs to come on Mondays already." Josh complained.

"Now, now, Josh. You know Mack would never do that. She aims to please and so should you. It's customers like Mrs. Dudley that help keep this place open for business."

"I guess." He grumbled.

He started working at the café a little less than a year after Mackenzie. He appeared to love his job but was content with being a full-time server and nothing more. In his spare time, he enjoyed working on classic cars and reselling specialty parts online. She often wondered why he never pursued going into business for himself, especially since he was so passionate about it.

Clara adjusted her chair at the front counter.

"Hi, Clara, what can I get for you today?" Chloe pulled out her notepad.

Chloe was a part-timer at the café and was in school studying culinary arts.

"Hey, Chloe. I think I'll take the special to go, and when you have a moment, could you tap Mackenzie on the shoulder for me? I'd love to have a quick word with her before I head out."

"Sure. One order of baked ziti coming right up, and I'll grab Mackenzie for you." She smiled.

HGTV was playing in the background on the big

screen and the place was buzzing with a bunch of end-of-day chatter. Across the café, Clara could barely see the side profile of a bearded man wearing sunglasses and a baseball cap that captivated her attention. She tried not to stare, but there was something about him that was familiar, yet eerie at the same time.

"Hey, girlie." Mack approached Clara from the other side and made her jump.

"Gee, are you all right? I didn't mean to startle you." Mack laughed.

Clara let out a brief sigh and gripped her chest.

"There must be something in the air today. First Mike got me, now you. Maybe it's me. I feel like I've been on edge lately, but there's absolutely no reason for it," she said.

"I'll tell you what it is. You're probably still adjusting to living by yourself in that sprawling beachfront mansion of yours. If I lived in a house that big by myself, I'd be on edge, too. You know what you need to do... you should call Mike to help keep you company at night." She teased.

"Shhh, keep your voice down. You're the only one that knows about-"

"Oh, Clara, please. At least half of Solomons have figured you two out by now. I wish you'd stop worrying so much about everyone's perception and let that man into your life completely before somebody else does." She interrupted.

"What are you afraid of? Who cares that he's your boss? Love is love, honey. You better open up your heart and let him in." Mack scolded.

"If I could get a word in edge wise... I am letting him in. In about a month he's opening up the new site on the northern end of the county. Once he relocates, then I'll feel more comfortable with... you know."

"Being an item? Good. It's about time. You deserve a good man in your life. You are so loving and the most humble woman I've ever met. Heck, you inherited a mansion and still drive an old Honda, and work when you really don't have to. If that isn't humble, I don't know what is," Mack said.

"Hey, don't talk about Bessy like that. I finally got her bumper fixed and polished her up. She still works like a charm." Clara defended her old car. She had to save up every penny to buy it and was proud to call it her own.

"I won't say another word about your precious car. Just remember you have a nice luxury sedan sitting in that garage and a boat out back that needs to be put to good use as well. I can't think of a better person to share all those things with than Mike."

"Ha, that boat will remain in honor of Joan, but you won't catch me touching it with a ten-foot pole. I get sea-sick just thinking about getting out there on the water." Clara chuckled.

Just then the eerie man walked by briskly and made his way out the door. Clara turned to get a good view of him, but only caught a quick glimpse from the rear. There was something about him. His hair line, his broad shoulders, and the cadence of his walk sent chills up her spine in a negative way.

"You all right?" Mackenzie asked again.

"Uh, yeah. Who was that guy? The one who just left."

"I've never seen him around here before. He's a strange bird if you ask me. It's the first time I've ever seen a customer sit in here with their sunglasses and a baseball cap on the entire time. As a matter of fact. Let me go over to his table and see if he left enough to cover his bill. I'll be right back. Can I get you anything from the kitchen?" Mack asked.

"Chloe already took my order. I was just popping in to grab something to go. Why don't you come by the house on Friday after work? Bring Stephanie with you. We can hang out on the beach. It will be fun."

"Oh, Stephanie would love that. It's a date."

Stephanie was McKenzie's smart and very independent first grader. She looked just like her mother and acted just like her as well. Some even said she's her mini-me. The two made a dynamic duo despite having an absent husband and father. He'd yet to make an appearance around Solomons Island, but it's been told that he was a deadbeat who took off to travel the world when Stephanie was just knee high to a duck. No one had seen or heard from him since.

"Looks like you got lucky, Clara. Chef just pulled

this fresh batch of ziti out of the oven. He put extra bread and parmesan in the bag for you." Chloe slid the brown paper bag in front of her.

"Mmm, it smells good. Is Chef Harold working tonight?" Clara asked.

"Of course, can't you tell by that delicious aroma?" Chloe laughed.

Clara paid for her meal and said her goodbyes for the evening and then left to head home.

She pulled into the cobblestone driveway of the place that still felt like Joan's home. It had only been about four months since she inherited the place from her former boss and friend, and with so much space, it felt like it would take an eternity to truly make it her own. In a lot of ways, Clara didn't mind preserving Joan's memory in the home. Especially in the library and the guests' bedrooms, and even the sunroom where Joan spent a lot of her time. It was her way of remaining close to her good friend.

She popped the trunk to remove a few bags and grab her baked ziti, but found herself distracted by a shuffling noise nearby. Clara turned to look, but there was nothing as far as she could see.

Maybe Mackenzie was right. Perhaps living in this big place all alone is getting to me, she thought to herself.

Clara scooped her things out of the trunk and swiftly made her way inside where she could close the door behind her and shake off any thoughts of fear.

She bent down to greet Holly, her dog, when her cell phone rang.

"Hey, Mike."

"I miss you," he said.

She let out a sigh of relief and smiled.

"Say it again, slowly, so I can take in every word of it."

"I...miss...you," Mike said.

"Mmm, those words sound like music to my ears. I miss you, too. But, we did just see each other about an hour ago." She teased.

"I know but it's not the same as being able to freely hold you and do all the things that lovers do."

"Is that what we're working toward? Being lovers?" Clara smiled, finding the conversation to be rather intriguing.

"I sure hope so. Until that day comes, I guess we'll have to wait patiently to find out."

"I guess," Clara said.

"Well, I just wanted to hear your sweet voice before we make it to our next stop on the tour. It's beautiful out here this evening, and it sort of has me thinking about how I want to take you out on another tour. Are you up for one last training session with the boss? I don't know that I'll have much time for it once I relocate to our new worksite."

"I'm always up for a tour with you, Mike."

"Good. Do you trust me?" he asked.

"Of course, I do."

"Then clear your calendar for this Saturday around five. I'll pick you up at your place. It's a total surprise, no questions asked."

"Okay, Mr. No Questions Asked. I'll see you on Saturday around five...and I'll see you at work tomorrow."

CHAPTER 2

On Thursday morning Mae woke up with Jonathan's arm wrapped around her waist as he cradled her in the spooning position. She turned around and smiled at the slightly opened position of his mouth as he slept like a baby. Sleeping over had become a frequent habit that normally resulted in driving to work together the next morning. Mae worked at Lighthouse Tours and showcased the county's five islands when clients hopped aboard her boat. Jonathan conducted fishing tours and occasionally brought home the catch of the day to share with his lady for supper. Today, Mae had to work an earlier shift.

"Jonathan... Jonathan, wake up," she whispered. "Huh?"

"Wake up, it's late, and I need to get going," she said.

"Mae, please. Five more minutes, love." Jonathan grumbled.

"I don't have five more minutes. We stayed in bed twenty minutes later than we should've to begin with."

"Mae, I'm tired for crying out loud. How often do I get to sleep in? It's not my fault you kept me up way past my bedtime." He complained.

"I kept you up? Oh, no, sir. That's nonsense and you know it. We always say we're going to play by the rules until one of us has a few glasses of wine, then that's all she wrote. Maybe we'll just have to go back to sleeping at our respective places at night," she said.

"Mae, is that what you really want? After we've come this far, you want to go backward and miss out on all this good lovin' in the morning?" Jonathan said as he threw the covers back and displayed his striped pajamas.

Mae laughed and tossed a pillow at him. They were a familiar couple, just a few months into the relationship, but with a friendship of over eight years, there wasn't much they didn't know about one another.

"No, of course, I don't want to miss out on all this lovin', but you and I can't seem to behave ourselves. I was late twice last week. Mike won't turn a blind eye to it forever. If we don't pull it together, eventually he's going to pull one of us by the coattail, and I refuse to let it be me," Mae said as she stood in front of the bathroom mirror brushing her teeth.

"Oh, so you'd rather me to be the one to get in trouble," he said playfully.

"No, I'm saying I don't want either of us to get in trouble. I heard he's installing one of those time machines for payroll before he leaves. I think we'll have to punch in and out every day, so we better get our act together now."

Jonathan slipped out of bed and approached Mae with his gentle hands to massage her shoulders. She pretended to remain focused on fiddling with her hair, knowing full well that each stroke from his hands was a sweet and sensual distraction.

She gave in, closed her eyes, and was overcome by the kneading of his hands.

"Why don't I stay here again tonight?" he whispered and then softly kissed her earlobe.

"Oh, Jonathan. Both of us need our rest. We're going to look like tired old rags for our clients during the day if we keep this up," Mae said.

"There's nothing about what we're doing that's tired or old, Mae. Nothing at all."

Mae grabbed a nearby wash cloth and whipped it at Jonathan's leg.

"Down boy," she said, pushing him away. "Now, get your clothes on and let's hustle. I'm leaving for work in ten minutes, and you have a nice bed waiting for you at home," she said.

Jonathan begrudgingly complied.

"About that. I know you're in a hurry, so maybe we can talk about it later on, but I think the two of us should take a serious look at our living arrangements. We see each other at least four to five nights a week. That might be an indicator that it's time to maybe... I don't know... merge somehow, or come up with some sort of arrangement so we don't have to keep going back and forth from your place to mine," he said.

"Jonathan, two stubborn old mules like us have no business talking about merging anything. I know exactly how I like to keep things around my place and you're the same way."

Mae slipped on her shoes and glanced at her knee brace, considering whether she should put it on. She was doing so well after her knee surgery. Using her cane had become more of a secondary thought, but she didn't want to overdo it.

"Since when did anybody start classifying the mid-sixties as old? I disagree with you, Mae."

Jonathan tilted Mae's chin toward him.

"You don't always have to be so stubborn about things, you know. I think you should give it some serious thought. And before you try to argue with me, I'm going to grab my car keys."

He kissed her eyebrow.

"Have a wonderful tour," he said as he exited the room.

Mae didn't have time to consider anything other than running behind schedule. She grabbed her earrings, shoved them in her pockets, threw her purse over her shoulder, and headed for the front door.

At Lighthouse Tours, Mike prepared his coffee and grabbed a legal pad to sketch his to-do list for the day. He greeted Clara professionally, determined not to breech their agreement, and said hello to a few of the other staff members as they arrived. Tommy was fairly new to the team but had a good handle on leading the boat tours and was ready to get out there on his own. Soon, he would replace all of Mike's tours as he prepared to open a new division of the business. Then there was Brody. He maintained the boats and had a newly gained responsibility of helping Mike purchase boats for the new location.

"Brody, you have a second? I'd like to sit down and go over a few options for the new fleet if you have time."

"I'm right behind you, boss. I jotted down a few notes after visiting the boat dealers yesterday." Brody pulled up a chair in Mike's office and flipped open his legal pad.

Mike closed the door and joined Brody at his desk.

"I hope you have some good news for me. We need at least two more boats to add to the fleet in order to successfully get up and running. With about a month left, I'm afraid we're cutting it close," he said.

"Not to worry, I got your back. I think this last place I visited had lots of potential. They have brand new options, but the owner also had at least a half a dozen contacts of people who were looking to sell their used boats."

"Yeah, but are we talking about quality boats that are in excellent condition?" Mike asked.

"The owner is willing to vouch for every person on the list. He said he only does business with the best, so you can take it for what it's worth. Look, the man has been in business just outside of Solomons for umpteen years now. That has to count for something. I looked up his store on the Better Business Bureau, and he looks like he's on the up and up to me. I think you should go check it out. With your mechanic, of course, yours truly." Brody slid the contacts list across the desk and waited for Mike's response.

"Brody, my man. You come through for me every time. I don't know how to thank you. If these contacts are any good, we could be well on our way to taking this business to the next level," Mike said.

"You can thank me by throwing in a raise. It's likely you're going to need me to help you maintain the boats at the new location, I would imagine. Or at least until you hire someone for that position." Brody smiled.

"You have a good point there. It's definitely a strong consideration. Let me just make sure I have my ducks in a row and everything is running smoothly with the new place. Then we can talk about a raise and perhaps even a promotion. I realize guys like you are hard to come by. You've been with me since the onset when we first started the operation back in Annapolis. I have to take good care of you and I will." Mike promised.

"I know you're good for it. How's things otherwise?" Brody asked.

"Oh, I'd say everything else is running pretty smoothly. The renovations are almost complete. I'm still interviewing for new staffers, but it's nothing I can't handle."

"That's good and all, but I'm talking about with you, personally. How's your folks? I haven't heard you say much about them lately. How's everything else? It seems like your addiction to work has increased since you decided to expand, but yet you also seem happier than ever. You know, that kind of happiness that only comes from meeting somebody special." He winked.

Mike put down his papers and rocked back in his chair with a slight smirk on his face. He suspected Brody was testing the waters to see how much he would say. The two went way back, so it wasn't uncommon to occasionally chat about women. But this time was different, so he remained nonchalant, while trying to figure out what Brody knew.

"Well, that was a loaded question. Let's see. For starters, my folks are doing well. They're still enjoying their place in Chesapeake and have no intentions of leaving as they like to remind me all the time. As for the ladies, I simply don't have the time, Brody. You've been around long enough to know how it is. Sometimes it feels like I'm here around the clock with barely enough time to eat," he said.

"Mike, I'm not buying it. As you say, I've been around long enough to know better. Somebody is giving you a little pep in your step these days, even if you don't want to admit it. I know it's not Savannah. You kicked her to the curb for good not long after Clara started working here. We all notice the way you smile at her."

"I do not know what you're talking about," Mike said.

"Come on, man. Save all that for the rest of the staff. I thought we were close." Brody adjusted himself in the chair.

"I won't press you if you don't want to talk about it, but just know you've never been a good liar, Mike. If you aren't seeing her, it's only a matter of time until you do."

Mike put his pen down and confessed.

"All right, look. I'm talking to you as Brody, my friend. Not as Brody who works here, you got it?" Mike asked.

"I got it. You know me by now. Your secret is safe with me."

"Good, because if you leak anything I'll know who to blame," Mike said.

"I said your secret is safe. Now spill it. What's up with you two?"

"I'm into her. Really into her. But she thinks it's best to wait until I start working out of the other office for us to make things more official, and although I hate it, I know it's the right thing to do." Mike admitted.

"Ahh, so I was right. You do have the hots for red." Brody tapped his fingers on the arm of his chair and laughed.

"Red? Is that what you call her?"

"Yeah, behind closed doors, of course. Honestly, I think it's a good thing. She seems to make you happy. I haven't seen you smile like this in such a long time. I was wondering if you'd ever meet someone who truly makes you happy," Brody said.

"Savannah and I made each other happy for a while."

"Mike, that was short-lived. And, that wasn't happiness. I'm sure she helped to keep you warm at night, but I always thought you could do better. No disrespect, but she wasn't exactly the type you could take home and introduce to the folks, if you know what I mean." He chuckled.

"Thanks, Brody. Tell me how you really feel," Mike said sarcastically.

"You didn't need me to say a word. All the single men with high-paying jobs on Solomons Island know about Savannah. But listen, enough about her. On to red. Are you two-"

"Are we what?"

Brody smiled big enough to reveal what was on his mind.

"Stop right there. I already know where you're going with this. Right now, we're just focused on keeping things professional at work and seeing where things lead once I leave here," Mike said.

"You want her, don't you?" Brody asked.

Mike hesitated.

"Is it that obvious? Man, I gotta hurry and get out of here, or I'm going to go stir crazy. I knew from the day I met her she was different. I should've never told her about the job, Brody. I mean, I wanted her to know about the job because she was searching, but-"

"You would've preferred getting to know her personally instead of working with her professionally," Brody said.

"Exactly!"

Brody stood up and adjusted his belt.

"Yep, you've got it bad, my brother. Whatever you do, don't overthink it. If you really like red, then give it time. It will work out. I tell ya, between you, red, and Ms. Mae and Jonathan, I'm feeling left out around here." Brody chuckled.

"Well, there's only one cure for that. Get out there and mingle. You can't expect to meet somebody by fixing boats all day and sitting at home drinking beer at night. Clean the grease off your pants and get out of the house every once in a while. It will do you some good."

"Yeah, yeah. I hear ya," Brody said.

"I can tell that just went in one ear and right out the other."

"Probably." Brody opened the door to leave.

"I'm free to check out the boats whenever you are," he said.

"All right, thanks, man."

When Brody left, Mike picked up a sponge ball and tossed it inside his miniature basketball hoop. It was his way of thinking things out when he needed to strategize for the business. Lately, in between strategic planning, all he could think about was Clara. The way her hair smelled, the taste of her lips, her hourglass shape, and the sweet sound of her voice sent chills up his spine just thinking about it.

CHAPTER 3

On Thursday evening Mack and her daughter Stephanie came over to grill and enjoy laying out on the beach. Holly completely captivated Stephanie and did everything with her, including dropping several hints that she wanted to take her home.

"Miss Clara, I can take care of Holly for you. She can come and stay at my house when you're busy. Dogs like to play with little kids, you know," Stephanie said.

"I'll have to keep that in mind, Stephanie. It sounds like you would be the perfect dog sitter should I ever need one." Clara laughed.

"You better watch her, Clara. She falls in love with the animals pretty quickly. If it were up to

Stephanie, we'd start our very own animal shelter in our one-bedroom apartment." Mack teased.

"Is that right, Stephanie?" Clara asked.

"Yes, ma'am. Dogs are my favorite, but I like little kitties, too."

"Little kitties, ferrets, birds. I finally had to draw the line at the idea of having a pet snake," Mack responded.

"Ooh, I don't blame you." Clara agreed.

"Ms. Clara, can I take Holly down to the beach to play frisbee? I promise I won't lose her." Stephanie begged.

"I know you won't. Holly is pretty good. She'll stay with you. It's fine with me if your mom says it's okay."

"Mommy, pleasssee?"

"All right. Go ahead, but you need to stay in this area where I can see you at all times, okay?"

"Okay!"

Stephanie grabbed the frisbee and charged off with Holly before her mother could think of any more rules. The sun was shifting, but there was still enough daylight left to enjoy a few rounds of frisbee before settling in for a nice grilled dinner.

"Clara, it's gorgeous out here. If this is what I had to come home to every night, I don't know that I'd ever want to leave. Would you look at this view? You have the sunset, a private beach-"

"It's not totally private. I can see the neighbors

when they're hosting parties or the kids are outside." Clara corrected Mack.

"Oh, whoopty doo. So, every once in a while you can see the neighbors who are several acres away... poor you! You get what I'm trying to say. This place is gorgeous and there's no denying it." Mackenzie teased.

"You're right. I still wonder what I ever did to deserve this. It blows my mind that Joan decided to completely exclude her family and put me in her will, instead. If this isn't a true rags-to-riches story, I don't know what is. But, you know what, Mack? The house, the boat, the cars, it means absolutely nothing if you don't have somebody to share it with."

Clara left the deck door open and began walking back and forth, serving appetizers and drinks while talking. She returned with her utensils and a plate filled with steaks to throw on the grill for dinner.

"Why don't you let me help you," Mack said.

"No, just relax and enjoy yourself. This is the easy part. Now, what was I saying?"

"You were talking about not being alone, but I have to tell you, Clara. I really see great things in your future. You just have to be patient and see where the road leads. Speaking of which, what are you and Mike up to this week? Have you been spending any quality time together?"

"We are, as a matter of fact. He's taking me on another one of his tours this Saturday. Let's be clear, he's not fooling anybody with these so-called tours. I'll admit that I was a hermit when I was working for Joan and needed to get out and see more of the island. And... it has improved my ability to speak with confidence when I'm making tour recommendations to clients. But, Mike is not fooling anybody. The tours are more like dates, if you ask me." Clara's voice said one thing, but her smile revealed she liked the idea of going on a date with Mike.

"Well, don't ask questions. Soak up every minute and have a good time. You deserve it. I mean, come on, Clara. When is the last time you've actually been with a man? I mean... really been with a man. Ten years?"

Clara's eyebrows folded like an old curtain.

"Exactly! You need to experience the love and touch of an experienced man who knows how to make your toes curl. Your time is long overdue," she whispered.

"Well, look who's talking. I'm not the only one who's rusty in the love-making department. If Stephanie is six years old, then I'll take a wild guess and say that you haven't been with a man in what... six years?"

Mack glanced over her fingernails and pretended to be concerned with how they looked.

"That's not the point. At the rate you're moving with Mike, I'll still be way ahead of the game. That man is caring, well-established, and hot as hell. What are you waiting for?" Mack asked.

"I don't disagree, but we're good. There's nothing wrong with taking your time. Especially when you find yourself in a unique situation like mine. Now, enough about me. What are we going to do about you? Are there any prospects in sight?"

"Maybe. It's nothing serious, but I met a guy at the café. His name is Bill. He's one of those lumber-jack types with a full beard and a little beer belly, but he's nice... easy to talk to and he seems to have taken a liking to sitting in my section and talking to me," Mack said.

"You with a lumberjack?" Clara asked.

"Yeah, why not? He's divorced but still very much a family man. He has a daughter that's heading off to her first year of college. He's good with his hands and he works over at the lumberyard."

"I don't get it. I always thought you were the suit and tie type," Clara said.

"Yeah, well, look where that got me. When I met Stephanie's father, he wore a suit and tie. Next thing you know, he was quitting his job and talking about starting a band and traveling the world. At least the lumberjack is settled and knows what he wants out of life." Mack laughed.

"How about that? Well, I hope to meet him some-time. I'll have to give him the best friend once over to make sure he meets my approval."

"Please do. He's been keeping your seat warm when you're not at the café. You can't miss him. The man lives in plaid shirts and always orders the same oven roasted turkey every single time." Mack sniggled.

"Hey, by the way, Clara. I meant to tell you that weirdo was back in the café again asking me about you last night. He didn't mention you by name, but he seemed awfully curious about who you were."

"Really? Me? That's odd. Did he say what his name was?".

"He said he goes by the name of Trent. Does that name ring a bell?" Mack asked.

"No. I don't know anyone by that name."

"That's strange. I thought maybe he was sweet on you with the way he was asking so many questions. I asked him if he knew you, but the only thing he said was that he'd seen you around before and was wondering what your name was. Of course, I didn't tell him. He could be crazy for all I know. I tried to find out some info about him, but the only thing he divulged is that he's staying with a friend. He was very vague, and he gave me the creeps."

Clara grew quiet. There was only one person she recalled from her past that could send a chill up her spine in a heartbeat. But she hadn't seen him in over ten years, so there was no point in considering him now.

~

On Saturday, at precisely five o'clock, Mike pulled up to the front courtyard of Clara's house in his jeep. He wore khaki shorts, docker shoes, and a gingham Vineyard Vines shirt that made him look irresistible.

Dear God, help me. How on earth am I supposed to keep my composure with him looking that good? she thought to herself as she peered out the front window.

She quickly put the curtains back in place and tugged on her dress to make sure she looked presentable. Clara had finally come around to buying new clothing and was particularly proud to have an array of options that didn't involve work clothing. As a kid growing up, she always had to recycle whatever she could to make it work for all occasions. This particular dress revealed a respectable sweetheart neckline and was soft and comfortable like a maxi dress.

The doorbell rang and as always Holly beat Clara to the door, announcing his arrival.

"Hey, Holly. How are you, girl?" Mike said as he stroked her fur.

When he looked up at Clara, he cracked a smile and his face turned flush.

"Hey," Clara said.

"Hi, you look amazing. Gosh, if I had known you were going to dress like that, I would've worn something else."

"It's just a cotton dress. Besides, you look great. Maybe if somebody would've told me where we were going, I could've dressed more appropriately," she said.

"No. What you're wearing is perfect for where we're going. Are you all set?"

"I think I have everything. Let me just grab my bag. You can come in if you'd like." Clara widened the opening of the front door, inviting him to enter the foyer.

"Wow, this place is phenomenal. I can't help but wonder what's a person to do with having this much space all to themselves?" Mike asked.

"Fill it with things that remind me of those that I love. And, maybe one day, adopt a whole baseball team or Girl Scout troop and give them a wonderful place to live," she responded.

"Would you really consider adopting some day?"

"The thought has crossed my mind. At my age I'm not really planning on having kids of my own, but it would be nice to fill the house with love and laughter. Giving a child a home might be a nice way to do that," Clara said.

She zipped her purse and placed the crossbody bag over her chest.

"Wouldn't you rather have someone to help you raise the child?" he asked.

"Ideally. I guess time will tell if it's supposed to come to fruition."

"You ready for our tour?" Mike extended his hand to Clara.

She placed her hand in his and followed him out the front door. She had to continually remind herself that they were keeping things platonic for a while longer and this was strictly an opportunity for her to get to know the island better.

Why wouldn't I want to brush up on my knowledge of the island? This way I can offer a better experience to the clients visiting Lighthouse Tours, she thought to herself.

Mike stopped in his tracks and looked Clara in the eye.

"I might not have a chance to be this close to you once we get to where we're going. Just one kiss, Clara, and I promise I'll behave myself for the rest of the evening," he said.

Clara looked at him as if she didn't believe a word of what he was saying, but played along, secretly desiring the kiss as much as he did.

She took a step forward and he met her the rest of the way. They teased each other with their lips, softly and blissfully playing with each other before pulling away.

"We better get going before we find ourselves in trouble, Mike Sanders."

He brushed her hair aside.

"I guess you're right."

On the ride to their outing, she considered how

foolish it was of her to think they wouldn't run into someone they knew. It's not like the island was so big that it could be avoided. Eventually they would be discovered, but she was already in his car and over the moon with excitement about the surprise he had in store.

"Mike, you know we're not fooling anybody but ourselves, right?" she asked.

"What do you mean?"

"This...what we're doing right now. This isn't on the job training as much as it is a date." Clara laughed.

"No, no.... I beg to differ. Our tours have provided you with invaluable experiences that you can use when dealing with our clients." He smiled while steering the jeep toward their destination.

"Mmm hmm, sure. Kissing being at the top of the list of importance, I suppose."

"Not so fast. We can keep the kissing between the two of us. No need to share that with the clients."

Clara's serious demeanor gave way to hearty laughter as she envisioned how terrible that would be.

"All right, on to more serious matters. Have you considered how you're going to physically keep up with the demands of running two places at once?" she asked.

"I have and I think I'm up for the challenge. I used to do it for quite some time when Kenny and I first started the Solomons store. I had my set days for being at each location before I finally settled in Solomons. I can't imagine why I won't be able to do it again."

"Yeah, but there were two of you to manage the workflow between the two locations. I would think this is a completely different animal. You're embarking upon the grand opening of something new that completely belongs to you. Isn't that kind of exciting, yet scary at the same time?" Clara said.

"Uh, it's exciting but not necessarily scary. At least, it hasn't been until now. You have me wondering if I should be more nervous than I am. To me, it's been helpful to have the prior experience, and it's super helpful that I'm opening up another business in the same exact industry. It's all about the location and drawing the customers in, really."

"Well, you seem really confident about it. I wish you nothing but success," Clara said.

"What about you? I know a lot has changed for you over the past few months. Are you still feeling pretty confident about wanting to continue at Lighthouse Tours?"

"Absolutely. I love my job. It gives me something to look forward to every day," she said.

"That's good. I'm just surprised with all the resources at your fingertips that you wouldn't want to branch out and start your own company. Maybe something in the housekeeping industry?" Mike asked.

"Trust me, the thought has crossed my mind, but not everyone is cut out to be an entrepreneur. I've come to discover that I'm more of a worker bee. My knowledge and experience when it comes to running a business is slim to none."

Mike had one hand firmly gripping the wheel and the other resting comfortably over Clara's hand.

"Well, then, you found the right guy. Stick with me and I'll teach you a few things."

~

They pulled into the parking lot of Nel's Art Gallery. It was off the beaten path of their usual type of excursions but still a welcomed change.

"An art gallery?" she asked.

"Yes, ma'am. Remember, the idea is for you to become well versed in knowing every little nook and cranny that the area has to offer. That way you can make suggestions to help meet our clients' needs, and you can speak from experience." Mike exited the jeep and came around to the passenger side to open the door.

"You see, some clients want to just take a boat ride and that's it. Some want to visit the historical sights and see the oldest lighthouse in the whole county, and others... they want to experience all that we have to offer by visiting places like the art galleries and the museums. An added bonus to coming on the first Saturday of the month is Nel's wine tasting event. That's what makes Lighthouse Tours unique. We're not going to just offer an hour boat ride and that's it. We're a full package deal. You want to go fishing, you got it. You want to go on a dinner cruise, we have you covered. You want to tour the island by boat? We can handle that, too," Mike said.

"Ahh, okay. I see where you're going with this. I like the concept a lot. It's just too bad I haven't been able to get over my sea sickness to actually enjoy the full extent of the tour."

He closed the door behind her and led her toward an illuminated path leading to the entrance.

"Don't worry, we'll work on that, too. There's plenty of over-the-counter medications that can help until you build up your stamina," he replied.

Inside there was a low symphony of music playing in the background and plenty of people mingling with a glass of wine in hand. It was the most sophisticated setting that Clara had experienced in all her time spent on the island.

"Wow, I didn't realize they had events like this out here," she said.

"Yeah, you have to give the island a little more credit. We're small but there's plenty going on to keep you from being bored," Mike said.

He led Clara to the first piece of art that was a

reflection of the surrounding area. It was a panoramic photo of the Patuxent with sand dunes from a nearby beach. Mike stared at it for a moment before moving on to observe the next painting.

As he continued to look straight ahead he said, "Clara, I hope you know that I'm starting to fall head over heels for you."

She was speechless.

"It's kind of taking me by surprise. I've never felt this way about anybody before. Especially someone that I've had to wait to be with," he said.

"Mike, surely you and Savannah were a hot item at one point. And, I'm sure you still have memories of your fiancé. Never is a pretty strong word."

"Again. I've never had strong feelings for a woman that I've barely dated. I stand by those words whole heartedly."

He invited her to get wine before continuing their tour of the gallery. As they mingled he kept his hands to himself as promised, but his words awakened all of her senses and allowed her to feel butterflies in the pit of her stomach.

"The process of waiting has only caused my feelings to grow even stronger. I want to continue to get to know you, Clara...every single part of you."

She cleared her throat.

"Wow, I wonder if you'll still feel the same after you get to know me. You know... after the thrill of waiting is over and the dust begins to settle," she said.

"I don't see why not. I'll probably want you even more."

For the remainder of the evening Clara had a difficult time focusing on anything other than wanting to end her sabbatical with being close to a man. She knew if anyone could help her achieve her goal it would be Mike. Still, she would tread carefully so as not to end up with a broken heart.

CHAPTER 4

*J*onathan had a friend, affectionately known as Dock, in the yacht business in Annapolis. Occasionally, he did side charter jobs for him to help during his busiest seasons. The extra money never hurt, but it was the fond memories of sailing those big beauties that made him commit to sharing it with his lady someday, if he ever had the chance.

Over the weekend, he made arrangements for a romantic Saturday night date with Mae. Their chartered boat would sail from Annapolis to Chesapeake Bay, and end with brunch back in Annapolis late Sunday morning.

"Sweetheart, this has been the best time I've ever had in my entire life. Being with you makes me feel so alive," Jonathan said.

He kissed her neck and continued pecking Mae all over to make her giggle uncontrollably.

"Jonathan, quit. You're tickling me." Mae sighed with a lingering smile.

"I have to agree with you. I've never experienced anything like this before. I still don't know how you pulled this off. I can see Dock loaning you one of his boats to cruise around for a couple of hours, but spending the night on a yacht, that's fancy living if you ask me," Mae said as she lay next to him.

"It's nice to get out and try something new every once in a while. If I didn't, we wouldn't be lying here witnessing the most beautiful sunrise I've ever seen."

Mae rolled over and drew the covers up and gazed out the window. With her back facing Jonathan, he took that as his usual invitation to snuggle up close from behind and hold her near.

"What's on your mind, Mae?"

"Just thinking about doing some gardening when we get back this afternoon. With all this rain and summer heat, those weeds have been popping up and sucking the life right out of my Zinnias," she said.

Jonathan lay in amazement. *Maybe this was poor planning on my part,* he thought to himself. *Maybe Mae is not a romantic sunrise kind of woman.*

Mae turned around.

"Oh, and by the way, did I ever tell you how nicely the bush you planted out front is growing? The woman at the nursery told me to plant Jobe's fertilizer sticks in the ground near the roots to promote healthy growth, but it's doing so well I don't see a need to bother with it," she said.

Jonathan retreated from his comfortable position next to Mae and laid back with his hands folded over his bare chest. He was beyond perplexed about everything Mae was thinking or feeling as of late. He thought they were doing well since deciding to be together, but something was off, and he was determined to get to the bottom of it.

"Jonathan? ... Jonathan, are you listening to me?" Mae asked.

"Yes, you were talking about fertilizer sticks. I heard you. What I can't help but wonder is what else is going on in that pretty little mind of yours?" he asked.

"What do you mean?" she asked.

"Mae, here we are in the middle of the bay on what I consider to be the most romantic overnight date that I've ever planned for us. I had to jump through hoops to make this date happen. The sun is rising, we're lying here together, and all you can seem to think about is your Zinnias. So, I want to know what's going on. Am I doing something wrong?"

"Nothing is wrong. Just because we don't have our hands all over each other every waking hour of the day doesn't mean something has to be wrong, Jonathan."

"If you say so. It just seems like lately you're enthusiastic about everything but us. If I'm contributing to that, I'd like to know." He argued.

"Jonathan, I don't know what would make you say such a thing. We're together all the time and I always make myself available to you."

"What about the conversation I wanted to have with you the other day about moving in together? You shied away from it on purpose," he replied.

"I didn't shy away from it. I was running late to work."

Mae turned over completely and nestled her body against Jonathan's.

"Look, sweetheart. Do we have to do this now?" she asked.

"I owe you an apology. I'm thankful that you planned something so special, and my timing with all the Zinnia talk was absolutely terrible. But, I promise I didn't mean any harm by it, and there's no underlying message behind it. You know me, Jonathan. I like my routines. I'm a simple gal from Solomons Island who likes her Sunday gardening, and sticks to the same schedule for meals and routines almost every day of the week. Please don't get upset with me for that," Mae said.

"I'm not upset with you. I knew those things about you before and I'm fine with it. I just would hope that every once in a while you'd be open to embarking upon new experiences with me, that's all." Jonathan snuggled closer.

"I have a new experience we can work on," she said.

"What is it?"

"Well, we have a few more hours left on this yacht. Our driver is probably fast asleep at this early hour. Why don't we have a little one-on-one time with a full view of the sunrise?"

"Now we're talking," Jonathan responded with his arms opened wide, fully ready to receive the woman who made his heart sing.

That same morning, Clara awoke to the sound of birds chirping outside her window. The forecast was calling for a high of eighty degrees on the first Sunday in June, and she couldn't wait to trek across the sand and hang out by her favorite spot on the beach. First, she would grab the Sunday news, which was usually waiting on her front doorstep, then take Holly out, and return to settle in with her favorite cup of hazelnut coffee.

"Come on, girl. Let's grab the news and go outside for your morning walk," she said while rubbing Holly's chin.

Clara whipped her hair into a bun, threw on the most comfortable clothing she could find, and listened to the sound of her flip-flops clapping down the staircase while making her way to the front door.

The Sunday news was on the front mat, as expected, with a piece of paper on top that read, "*Clara.*"

That's interesting. Perhaps the delivery person left a note for me, she thought.

She grabbed the paper with the note and walked Holly to her designated area to take care of her business. While she waited for Holly, Clara opened the note and read the words.

"*It's been a while, but we both knew this day was coming. We have some unfinished business to discuss. Meet me at the Patuxent park at three o'clock. I'll be waiting on the bench near the entrance. Come alone. Keith.*"

Clara's heart sank. She slowly crumbled the paper in her hands and then more rapidly, balling it until the paper was barely recognizable. It had been ten long years since she'd seen Keith. She remembered the morning she left him just like it was yesterday. She pre-packed the essential items she would need for her road trip the night prior. She prepared his meal before going to bed, and that morning, once he left for work, she got in her car and drove right out of his life for good. The note she left on the kitchen table explained she was seeking a fresh start and that she wasn't returning to such a verbally abusive marriage. She made two final stops that morning. One to the social security office to fill out paperwork to switch back to her maiden name, and the second stop was by her sister's house, which

43

resulted in one last blowout over her parents' benefits after their accidental death. When she left the state of New York, she vowed if she ever returned, it would be under better circumstances that didn't involve a controlling husband or fighting with her sister over money. Since then, Maryland had been Clara's home. A place where she established a new life free of turmoil.

Is he seeking a finalized divorced? she thought.

I should've handled that years ago. She paced around while trying to figure things out.

The mere fact that he made it all the way to my doorstep means that he's been researching everything about me. I'll be damned if I'm going to allow him to slither back in and try to control me. Come on, Clara, you've got to think of a plan that doesn't involve meeting him at the park.

She waited for Holly to finish, looked around to ensure they were alone, and returned to the house. She slammed the door behind her and secured the double locks. After setting the alarm, she frantically dialed Mack's number at the café.

"Thank you for calling the café. This is Mackenzie speaking."

"Mack, this is Clara. Do you have a minute?"

"I have five minutes for you, Clara, but why on earth are you whispering?" she asked.

"I don't know. Listen, remember that guy that came in the café with the baseball cap... you know, the one who was asking questions about me and sort of creepy acting?" she asked.

"Yeah, funny you should mention it. He's been sitting at the booth by the window for at least ten minutes now. He just put in a breakfast order. I figured if he was going to ask me about you today, I was going to be blunt and tell him a thing or two. Do you think you know him?"

"I can't be certain. I never caught a good glimpse of his face, but there was something about him that was very familiar. What color were his eyes?" Clara asked.

"It's kind of hard to tell with the way he's wearing his cap. He keeps his head down most of the time, but if I had to guess, I'd say they were a dark brown color."

"What about his tooth? If memory serves me right, he has a chipped tooth on the bottom row that can't be missed when he talks... unless he got it fixed," Clara said.

"He has a chipped tooth. Clara, you're making me nervous. Why do you know so much about this guy and who is he to you?"

"Trust me, it's a long story. One that I've never shared with anybody and will probably shock the heck out of you if I tried to explain it now. Look, I need you to do me a favor. I'll explain everything later, but for now, can you do your best to make sure he doesn't leave? I'm coming over to pay him a brief visit under my terms."

"Sure, but I don't have a good feeling. Are you certain this is a good idea?" Mackenzie asked.

"Mack, just make sure he doesn't leave. Please. I'll be there in about twenty minutes."

~

Clara walked into the café about twenty minutes later as scheduled. Mackenzie nodded her head toward the booth where the strange man sat during his last few visits to the café. She caught a glimpse of him from the back, wearing the same baseball cap, and looking at a newspaper while eating his food.

She approached him from behind.

"What do you want, Keith?"

He rested against the back of his seat and raised his coffee mug, taking a sip. Then he turned around to greet Clara with a wet grin on his face.

"Well, well, well. Look who it is. Miss Clara Covington, in the flesh. Except you're early. Let me guess... did your little waitress friend call you?" he asked.

"No. Actually, it was the other way around. I thought I recognized you when you were in here the other day. You might want to work on the disguise. It's not working so well for you," she said.

46

"Please, have a seat. It's been a while. Let's catch up."

"I'm not here for small talk, Keith. What's with leaving the note at my front door?" she asked.

"So, it is your front door? Wow, pretty swanky place you have there. How'd you get to be so lucky?"

"What... do... you... want... Keith?" Clara asked in a snarky tone.

"Well, at least sit down and act like you want to have a conversation with me. That way folks won't start staring."

She sat down cautiously, leaving her purse gripped at her side.

"I don't have intentions of meeting you at the park. Tell me what you want so I can get on with my life," Clara said.

"Oooh, you don't have to be so nasty. I've stayed out of your hair for what, ten years now? The least you could do is pretend to be nice. It wouldn't hurt to show me a little hospitality. I mean, I am still your husband and all."

Clara was disgusted at the thought of ever calling him husband.

"About that. I think it's long overdue that we finalize the divorce, and I'm sure you would agree," she said.

"Not so fast, pretty lady. You weren't in a hurry before today. I haven't considered remarrying, and clearly you haven't either, so what's the rush? Besides, I received a nice little notice in the mail that states we have some money in the bank... it said something about an inheritance. Thought I'd look you up and come see for myself what the fuss was all about. I had no idea I'd find you living in a sprawling mansion. You sure hit the jackpot."

"Oh, so that's what this is about. Go figure. Well, I'm not sure why you would still receive any of my mail, but you can rest assured there's nothing here for you, and I do mean nothing," Clara said.

"That's not what the law says. We're married, remember? It takes more than just changing your last name to undo fourteen years of marriage, sweetheart. What's yours is mine and what's mine is yours."

"You're even more of a creep than you were the day I left you. Whatever hole you crawled out of to find me, do yourself a favor and go back in it. I'll call my lawyer and see that the papers are drawn up immediately. Goodbye, Keith."

As Clara got up, he grabbed her by the wrist. In a few swift maneuvers across the floor, Mackenzie was at their table looking to assist.

"How's everything over here? Can I get you a refill, sir?" Mack asked while looking at Clara.

He eased his hands off Clara and relaxed in his seat.

"I wouldn't mind having another cup. Perhaps the lady would like to stay awhile and order something for breakfast," Keith said.

Clara tried to give Mackenzie a reassuring nod to help put her mind at ease. Keith was a scumbag, but he wasn't crazy enough to pull any stunts in public. Even when they were together, his worst behavior consisted of hurling negative insults and trying to intimidate her. He wasn't much for physical abuse, but who knows if that had changed over the years.

"It's all good, Mack. I was just about to leave," Clara said.

"Nah, why don't you hang out a little while longer so we can catch up? It will be just like old times."

Clara signaled Mack that it was okay to get the coffee. Once Mackenzie walked away, she glanced over her shoulder, looking suspicious.

"Here's how this is going to work. I'm going to get up and walk out of here. In just a short while, you'll be served the divorce papers in New York, and then we'll be done with this nightmare of a marriage once and for all. Don't come to my house again and don't bother trying to get my telephone number. You got it?" Clara said while raising up from her seat.

"Geesh. Somebody woke up on the wrong side of the bed this morning," he said.

"Have a nice life, Keith."

Clara stormed away, feeling proud that she beat him at his little game and partially afraid that this wasn't over.

Back in the car, she waited about ten minutes before calling Mack. The skeleton Clara buried in the closet years ago had reared its ugly head right before Mackenzie's eyes. The least she could do was fill her in and help put her mind at ease.

How in the world am I going to explain this? she thought.

"Hey, Josh," Clara said.

"There you are. You took off so fast I didn't have a chance to say hello to you. Girl, if I didn't know any better, I would've thought someone was chasing after you."

Clara cleared her throat.

"Is Mack around?"

"She's wrapping things up with a customer. Hold on a moment."

While on hold Clara pulled into her driveway and clicked the remote to her garage door, which wasn't something she normally did. There was something that felt secure about hiding her car inside and allowing the door to close behind her before getting out.

What am I doing? Am I really going to let him scare me like this? she thought.

"Clara?"

"Mack." She sighed.

"Would you mind telling me what's going on? I was giving you five more minutes to call me back and if you hadn't, I was going to come looking for you. What the heck, Clara?"

"I know. I promise it's not as bad as it looks. He looks rough around the edges, but he's harmless."

"Why don't you start by telling me who he is?"

After a period of silence, Clara continued.

"Is he still there?" she asked.

"No, he left minutes before you called. Who is he?" Mackenzie pressed further.

"He's my husband."

"What?" Mackenzie said.

"He's my husband. We were married four miserable years prior to me leaving New York. By the time we met, I had buried that part of my life, never to talk about it again. He devalued me as a human being. He verbally abused me and almost made me believe I was losing my mind. I became a recluse and lost most of my friends. He even tried to create distance between me and my sister. Although that took little effort because our relationship was already pretty damaged. I hung around until I couldn't take it anymore. Then one day... I left. I changed back to my maiden name, packed my things, said goodbye to my sister, and left."

"Clara. Oh my, I'm so sorry. What a heavy burden to carry around for so long."

"You don't have to apologize. I just thought I should tell you. I didn't want you to be worried after what happened earlier," Clara replied.

"Why is he here after all these years?"

"Somehow he received information about the inheritance, which I find to be absolutely ludicrous. I've been living here long enough that all of my mail comes to me here in Maryland. It doesn't make sense," she said.

"Oh, no. Tell me this is not what I think it is."

"It's probably worse than what you're thinking. But I have it under control. Keith is more talk than anything else."

"I don't know, Clara," Mack said sounding discouraged.

"It's fine. I'm going to do exactly what I should've done ten years ago, which is file the divorce papers and be done with him. Maybe then, I can actually move on with my life in peace."

CHAPTER 5

*M*onday morning couldn't come soon enough for Clara. She tossed and turned, worried about what Keith may plan to do next. After finally drifting off, well after the midnight hour, she needed a strong cup of coffee to help keep her eyes open at work.

"My head hurts and it feels like I've been hit by a Mack truck," she said.

Ms. Mae plopped a bottle of Tylenol on Clara's desk, hard enough to make its contents rattle.

"What's the matter? You have a hangover?" Ms. Mae asked.

"No. I just didn't get enough sleep, that's all."

"Ooh, so you had some company over last night." She smiled and pointed toward Mike's office.

"No, Ms. Mae. I did not have company over. I

just had a hard time getting to sleep, that's all. What about you? Did you have company over last night?" Clara pointed toward the back of the building where Jonathan normally worked on the boats.

"I had company all weekend. Jonathan planned an overnight stay on a yacht. It was our own little romantic getaway. Just the two of us." She boasted.

"Wow, you two have really been hitting it off well. I guess soon you'll be making wedding plans." Clara suggested.

"Nah. That's not our style. We're close and we love each other, but we've also been friends for so long. I can't imagine we'd just turn everything upside down after all these years," Mae said.

"Why would you view it as turning everything upside down? If you love each other, then one would think you'd be sealing the deal... joining worlds, if you will. That's not a bad thing if you're doing it with the right person."

"Ha. Clara, Jonathan and I are like... well-oiled machines. Everything is running smoothly just the way it is. Sometimes in life, when you make too many changes, you take the risk of upsetting the apple cart. We're getting older now. He's set in his ways and I'm set in mine. His routine is exactly the same every single evening. First, he puts on his pj's, then he goes through his whole dental routine, then he has to turn the television on at the same precise time to hear the nightly news every single evening. I'm the complete opposite. I like to be quiet at night and get into a good novel before going to bed. I also can't stand the smell of burned toast in the morning... and let me tell you. This man has literally burned toast just about every morning since we've been together." Mae looked around to see if anyone was coming before she continued.

"The other thing that's wearing me out is missing out on my beauty rest at night. Again, I love the man, I really do. But a woman needs her rest at night so she can feel refreshed and not so cranky the next morning," Mae said.

"So, just tell him you're tired and want to head to bed earlier, that's all."

"You try telling that to a man once his special pills have kicked in." She winked.

Clara spit her coffee all over the front desk just in time for Jonathan and Brody to come in from the dock.

The gentlemen brought the scent of the river with them, carrying in fishing rods and tools from the boat. Clara gently patted a paper towel over her documents and wished the two men a good morning.

"Good morning, guys. I was thinking about picking up some bagels from the café. Anybody interested in placing an order?" she asked.

"Morning, Clara. I'll take an everything bagel with cream cheese, if you don't mind," Jonathan said.

"Make that two everything bagels with cream cheese," Brody added.

"Ms. Mae, do you want anything?" Clara asked.

"No, I think I'll pass this time. I need to work on my girlish figure. It seems with every new year that passes, I'm slowly but surely growing a tire around my waistline."

"Okay, let me check with Mike then. Does anybody know if Tommy is scheduled to come in today? I don't see his name on the chart, but I could've sworn Mike said he'd be in today."

"He'll be here shortly. He had some family business to take care of this morning," Brody responded.

Mike emerged from the back with a stack of papers in hand.

"Ahh, all of my favorite people gathered in one place. Perfect. I was thinking about holding an impromptu meeting to go over a few updates about the new location. Everybody free to meet in about about an hour before the first tour heads out for the day?" he asked.

"That works for me, boss," Jonathan replied.

The rest nodded in agreement.

"Great, that way Tommy can join in as well."

"Clara, are you feeling okay? You don't seem like your usually peppy self," Mike said.

"Just a little tired, that's all. It's nothing coffee and a warm bagel won't cure. Do you want anything? I'm going to pick up an order to go," she said.

"Sure. A plain bagel with butter works. Thanks."

It seemed like whenever Mike spoke to Clara in the office, one by one the staff cleared out, making excuses to leave the room. Clara assumed it was an unspoken rule they shared, secretly knowing her and Mike had feelings for one another.

"There they go, clearing out the room again. It's becoming rather comical if you ask me," Mike said.

"I don't get it. We're pretty good about keeping things strictly professional around here," she replied.

"Yeah, until I catch you in the supply room. Then all bets are off." Mike teased.

"Hey, why don't you let me pick up those bagels for you. Stay here and relax. You have a bottle of Tylenol on the desk and a cup of black coffee in hand. That can't be good," he said.

"No, it's okay. I don't mind-"

"Clara, don't be stubborn. It's nothing for me to hop across the street and pick up the bagels. Let me take care of you," he said.

She gave in. Originally, she was planning to steal away and talk to Mackenzie. She needed to rehash the events of the prior day and come up with a game plan. But, for now, her head was throbbing, and she was tired, so she gave in to Mike's request.

～

Mike approached the front counter at the café, nodding at a few of the patrons who were known for lingering after the morning rush. He sat beside an unfamiliar man who barely grunted while burying his face in a newspaper. Chloe was wiping down the glass windows, while Josh approached the front counter with a brown paper bag in hand.

"Mike, my man, how's it going?" Josh said.

"Aww, you know how it is. Busy as usual."

"Hey, where I come from, that's a good thing. If you're busy, that means you're putting food on the table," Josh replied.

"I can't argue with that."

"All right, let's see. I have two everything bagels with cream cheese and one plain bagel with butter. If I know right, the plain belongs to you." Josh smiled.

"You know me well, my friend. Would you mind throwing in some jelly packs, just in case? Also, I hate to be a pain, but maybe I can place a side order for Clara. Maybe scrambled eggs and sausage links or whatever you have back there that's suitable for a headache. She's not feeling well this morning, so I thought I'd bring her back something with substance," Mike said.

The gentleman sitting next to him cleared his throat and put down his paper. Mike gave him a nod to say hello, observed his appearance, and kept talking to Josh.

"Sure, no problem. So, how's it going with you and Miss Covington?" Josh asked.

"Well, if you're asking how is everything going at the job, I'd say everything is working out great. She's highly efficient and everybody loves her. What more could I ask for?" Mike responded.

By this time Mike noticed the guy sitting next to him was staring at his reflection in the mirror. It was a little awkward, but he pushed past it and ignored him.

"Mike, come on, you know what I mean. This town is not stupid. Everyone knows that you two are a match waiting to happen. According to Mack and the others, you haven't been the same since Clara walked into Lighthouse Tours. I saw the extra pep in your step and smile on your face when you walked across the street. Somebody is in love." Josh grinned.

Mike tried to suppress an enormous smile.

"What else has Mack and everyone else been saying? I sure would like to know. Maybe it would give me some more insight into what Clara's thinking," he said.

"Ahh, so you care about what she thinks. Mmm hmm, I knew it. It's only a matter of time," Josh said.

"You're just as bad as the rest of the town gossips, Josh."

"Oh, no. Not me. Your secrets are safe with me. Let me put this order in and I'll be right back."

Mike peeked inside the brown paper bag and

folded everything back up to maintain the hot fresh aroma. He noticed the strange man still sipping his coffee and occasionally glancing at him.

"Hey there, have we met before?" Mike asked.

"No, I don't think we have. Although, I will say you look like somebody I know."

"I get that all the time." Mike extended his hand.

"I'm Mike Sanders, and you are?"

"Keith." He returned the handshake

"Nice to meet you, Keith. I would imagine you're new around here," Mike said.

"Yes, I am, actually. Just visiting, though. Sounds kind of silly, but I'm in town trying to rekindle an old flame. I didn't mean to pry, but when I heard you and the young fella talking about your lady friend, I found it to be kind of motivating. There's nothing like having the right one by your side. Somebody to keep you warm on those long cold nights." He chuckled.

"Yeah, well, I'm long past the days of just wanting someone to keep me warm at night. That has its perks, but it won't keep you together when times get rough. There's nothing like building a solid foundation together," Mike said.

"You sound like a pretty wise guy. I'm sure things will work out just fine for you."

"Thanks, man. You as well. Hey, if you and your lady are interested in taking a romantic tour of the island, stop by Lighthouse Tours. We're right across the street. Come and pay us a visit sometime. If I'm not there, my assistant, Clara, will take good care of you." Mike offered.

"Clara, right. The one with the headache."

Mike hesitated and then smiled. From the sound of things, this guy was listening in on his entire conversation and was quite observant.

"Yeah, that's her."

Just then Josh returned from the kitchen with his extra order in hand.

"You're in luck. Chef was already scrambling some eggs, and his links were hot and ready to go. Chef told me to tell you this one is on the house. Clara already took care of the bagels over the phone," Josh said.

"Are you sure? I don't want you guys getting in trouble with the boss."

"The owner is cool. He encourages us to take good care of our repeat customers," Josh replied.

"No, I'm talking about the real boss, Mackenzie." Mike laughed.

Mike said his goodbyes and spoke to Keith one last time before heading out the door.

"Nice to meet you. Good luck with your situation," he said.

"Likewise," Keith responded.

～

MICHELE GILCREST

Back at the store, Clara sat alone at the front desk massaging her temples. She wore blue light glasses to help reduce the strain of staring at the screen and looked desperate for relief in the form of food.

"Mike, thank you for picking up the bagels. My head is giving me a fit. I'm so desperate for something to eat I was about to call the café and ask what was taking so long," she said.

"That would be my fault." Mike made sure no one was coming. He laid the food down and began massaging Clara's temples.

He eased down to the lower portion of her neck, applying pressure with both hands, dragging his fingers slowly to her scalp. It was a technique he learned years ago when his fiancé used to suffer from migraines. He repeated this process a few times, responding to her as she let out a quiet moan.

"That feels so good," she whispered. His hands were so strong, yet loving. It sent chills down her spine.

Mike gently kissed the top of her head and shifted his focus on unpacking the food.

"Okay, I'll see that everyone gets their bagels. Here's a little something extra to help you feel better," he said.

"Aww, what is it?"

"Scrambled eggs and sausage to go with your bagel. You need a hardy breakfast instead of just eating bread. Eat up. We'll all meet in the conference room in about an hour," Mike said as he headed to the back.

"Thank you," she said, and began digging in.

She sank her teeth into her bagel and then washed it down with a sip of coffee.

Not even halfway through her meal, she looked up to see her worst nightmare walking through the front door.

"There you are, baby. I've been searching all over for you since your abrupt little exit yesterday." Keith grinned.

Clara checked over her shoulder, feeling relieved that no one was within earshot of their conversation.

"What are you doing here? And how the heck did you find out where I work?"

"It wasn't all that difficult. All you gotta do is hang out with the locals for a little while and you can learn a lot. I heard you found yourself a little boyfriend. What's his name? Mike?" Keith snarled.

"Where is he? I bet he'd be pretty surprised to see that I came to pay him a visit so soon," Keith said in a threatening tone.

"Never mind about where he is. You have no business coming by my job like this."

"Clara, you are my business. You're my wife, re-member? If you don't want me to make a spectacle out of you here at the workplace, then follow me out-side so we can talk," he said.

Clara carefully considered her options. She put

her fork down and watched Keith as he reached over the counter and grabbed a sausage off her plate.

"Tasty." He turned around and signaled for her to follow him outside.

He crossed over to the other side of the road and faced Clara with his hands tucked in his pockets.

"Isn't it so much nicer when we cooperate with each other?" he asked.

She didn't respond.

"Now, to pick up where we left off, I think it's only right that you share a portion of your new-found wealth with me. I mean, with all the pain and suffering you caused by walking out on the marriage, it's the least you can do. At least, that's the way I'd paint it to the judge once you serve the divorce papers. I'll tell him about all the emotional damage that was caused due to the abandonment. I've been thinking long and hard about it, and I think with the help of a lawyer, I could build a decent case. Decent enough to get the court system to force you to pay half of your inheritance."

"You creep. You wouldn't dare," she said.

"Oh, you don't know me well enough, my dear. Times are rough right about now, and I'll do whatever it takes. The way I see it, you're better off negotiating a fair share with me rather than being forced by the courts to split half. What's Maryland state law say? I think it's once you've been married seven years, any assets acquired after the marriage have to be equally divided between the two parties. Ha! If I were you, I'd much rather negotiate, let's say, twenty percent."

"Twenty percent? You must be out of your mind, Keith."

"As looney as they come. I can aim for thirty percent if that suits you better," he said.

"You son of a-"

"Now, now. Let's be sweet to each other. No need for harsh words. Twenty-five percent and I'll put my John Hancock on those divorce papers so fast it will make your head spin." He offered.

She dug her nails into her palms and clenched to keep from losing control.

"Here's what we're going to do. Your little work crew is starting to gather by the front window. I'm sure Mikey boy is curious to know why you're talking to me. I'll give you until mid-week to withdraw the funds. Have everything ready for me in a bag by Wednesday evening. I'll meet you at your place. After that, I'll sign the papers with no strings attached, and you'll never hear from me again," he said.

"This isn't right, Keith. This isn't right and you know it."

He glanced across the street and then brushed his hand along Clara's cheek. They were standing in broad daylight, across from the store, and steps away from the café where they could be seen by everyone.

"Life isn't always fair, baby cakes. I felt the same way when you walked out on me. I longed for these sweet lips, but you were nowhere to be found." Keith firmly placed his hands around Clara's waist, pressing her into his body, and kissed her. He tried to hold her but she pushed him away, trying not to cause a scene. When she turned around, she could see Mike standing in the window of Lighthouse Tours, looking crushed.

"If you say anything to your little friend at the diner or Mikey boy, the deal is off. I'll take this thing to the courts and squeeze every last dime out of you." He turned her chin toward him, attempting to kiss her one last time, but she turned her head and walked away.

CHAPTER 6

Jonathan dragged the two rocking chairs on Mae's front porch beside one another. He patted the cushion on the chair, inviting her to join him. Early evenings in June on Solomons Island were typically in the upper sixties, sunny, and the street was filled with kids from the neighborhood buzzing up and down on motorized bikes.

"When I was a kid growing up, we rode regular bicycles that required you to pedal your feet. Today, these kids buzz around on these expensive bikes... you ought to see the price tag on those things. I don't know how parents keep up. I can barely keep up as a grandparent." Mae complained.

"How are the grandkids?" Jonathan asked.

"They're doing well. Everybody is talking about coming down for the Fourth of July. I was thinking about asking my sister, Rose, to join us. You should invite your sister, Andy, and her husband to come and spend some time with us as well."

"They may travel as they normally do around the fourth, but I'll say something to her."

"It's been so long since I've seen Andy. I hope they can come," Mae said.

"What do you want me to tell them about us?" Jonathan asked.

"What do you mean? Tell them we're planning a little get together for the fourth and we'd love to have them come visit," Mae responded.

"No, that's not what I mean. Naturally, Andy will be curious about our status. I can imagine her and her husband will stay at my place, but we'll come over during the day. What should I tell them?"

"Jonathan. Aren't you overthinking this a bit? The last time Andy was here, you brought her over. What's the big deal?" Mae said.

"It's different this time. You and I are together now. You don't think she'll be the least bit curious about us?" he asked.

"So, why don't you say something ahead of time? That way she doesn't have to wonder. Honestly, Jonathan, I don't know what's gotten into you lately. Is everything okay?"

Jonathan propped up in his chair and faced Mae.

"I'll tell you what's gotten into me, Mae. It irks me to see how casual you are about us. It really does.

I waited a long time to be with you, and when we finally came together, you seemed to want this relationship. Now, I'm not so sure. It's the subtle things that catch my attention the most... you like your routines, you're making it clear that we do better living on our own. The only time you don't complain is when we're intimate, but even that is starting to feel different. Just come out with it, Mae. Tell me how you're really feeling and be done with it." Jonathan begged.

Mae stared toward the front yard.

"I feel like it was a huge undertaking for me to embrace the idea of being in a relationship, after my husband died. It took a long time for me to arrive at a place where I wanted to open my heart. But I finally did it. That may not be enough progress for you, Jonathan, but it's a big deal to me," she said.

"Mae, I mean this in the most respectful way, but it has been at least eight, going on nine years now. Since then, we've developed a best friendship that had blossomed beautifully. I don't want to pressure you, but I can't help but wonder if this is as far as you'll ever go. I want more, Mae. I desire to have it all with you. Returning to an empty home after being with you is starting to feel lonely," Jonathan replied.

"So, what are you trying to say? If we don't live together, you don't want to do this anymore?" she asked.

"What is this? Can you even define what this is?

We're two best friends that fell in love, or at least I did. I've been in love with you for a long time. But I don't want to shack up with you, Mae. I want more," Jonathan replied.

For several moments all that could be heard was the sound of the bikes buzzing back and forth and children playing.

"I'm not going to give you an ultimatum, Mae. But, I'm also not going to do this forever. I... deserve more. We deserve more."

A teardrop rolled down Mae's face as she continued to look everywhere but into Jonathan's eyes. She quickly patted her face dry.

"Maybe we need some time apart. You know, to sort things out," she said.

"I don't need time, but if you do, I can respect that. You know where to find me."

Jonathan grabbed his cap and slowly walked down Mae's front walkway to his pickup truck. With each step, he hoped Mae would change her mind and call him back. He turned and looked at Mae once more, but neither of them said a word.

The next morning Mike held a meeting with the staff. He gave an excuse for canceling it the day before, which Clara wasn't buying. Mike's demeanor was unusual... much more distant and reserved. His phone went directly to voicemail when she tried calling the evening prior, and he didn't make time for small talk today as he normally would.

"Hi, Mike," Clara said.

"Good morning, Clara. If you wouldn't mind letting the staff know that we're meeting in ten minutes in the conference room, that would be great," he responded.

"Don't you want to talk about it?"

"Talk about what?" he said.

"Yesterday. I know you saw me talking to that man across the street yesterday. You were in the window."

"You don't owe me any explanations. What you do and who you decide to talk to is your business." He placed a pen above his ear and made himself busy, pretending not to be concerned.

"We need to talk. It's not what you're thinking at all," she said.

"I'm not thinking anything. I'm good. Right now, the only thing I'm focused on is this meeting and a full day ahead. I'll see you in a few." He placed a sign in the front window and returned to his office.

That conversation went well, she thought.

She walked over to the front window and read the sign that said, "*Grand Opening of Our New Store Location This Weekend.*"

Her heart sank. He achieved his goal, which

made her happy, but it also meant he was leaving sooner than expected.

Clara made a brief announcement on the PA system, which could be heard out back by the dock. *"Lighthouse staff meeting begins in the conference room in ten minutes."* She then grabbed her mug with the letter C on the front for a refill on her coffee.

Jonathan popped his head in.

"What's the meeting all about?" he asked.

"If I had to guess, I would imagine it's about the new location. Read the front sign." She pointed toward the window.

He walked over and positioned himself to see what the fuss was about.

"Ahh, makes sense. Okay, well, I was hoping to get out and purchase some new equipment this morning. Guess I'll have to delay that until later," Jonathan said.

When Ms. Mae resurfaced from the back, Jonathan excused himself.

"Clara, I'm going to make myself comfortable in the conference room. I'll see you soon."

"Okay, I'll be right behind you," she responded, noticing that he said nothing to Mae.

Mae's expression was one of disappointment as she watched Jonathan pass her by. Clara chose not to pry. She had enough problems of her own, including how to make it through this meeting without encountering another awkward exchange with Mike.

~

"Good morning, everyone. I apologize for having to reschedule our meeting. I won't take up too much of your time, but I thought it was important that I share important updates as I receive them."

Brody, Tommy, and Jonathan sat closest to Mike while Clara and Mae sat on the far end of the table.

"As you all know, one of my primary goals was to get Tommy trained and up to speed so he could take over my boat tours. He's successfully been able to do so; therefore, I feel good loosening the reins and allowing him to take over my shift. In the next coming weeks, I'm going to make sure we get a couple of part-timers in here to ensure that I cover all shifts, should any of you call out sick. Right now the schedules are staggered enough where this shouldn't be much of an issue, but I still think the additional support is a good idea."

As Clara took notes, it looked as though everyone nodded in agreement.

"Now, on to my big announcement. Our north beach location is opening up this weekend. It's a few weeks earlier than expected, but we're ready, and I'm excited about this opportunity. During the first full week I'll be in North Beach, and then after that I'll start my new schedule, which will require me to split half my time at each location. Clara will have the details of my schedule, and as always, you can reach me on my cell if anything comes up that's a pressing issue."

Mike laid his pen and pad down and opened up the next portion of the meeting for questions.

"In no way am I telling you how to do your job, Mike. I'm still the new kid on the block, but have you considered hiring someone to help you with admin responsibilities?" Tommy said.

"Well, Tommy, after careful consideration, I don't think it will be necessary to hire somebody completely new. However, I am considering splitting some responsibilities with one of you. I guess that would be another important item to add to the agenda of our next monthly meeting. Great question, Tommy. I'm also looking at using Brody's mechanical expertise at both locations. So, if there are days when he's not at this shop, he'll likely be with me. Anybody else have questions?" Mike asked.

"Congratulations, Mike. I know this has been a long time in the making for you. You deserve it. I wish you all the success," Jonathan said.

"My sentiments exactly." Brody agreed.

The women in the room smiled in agreement but did more listening than speaking.

"Thanks, guys. I'll keep you posted should anything else change in the next few days. If there are no other questions, then I think we can wrap things up," Mike said.

One by one everyone filed out of the meeting,

leaving Clara, still sitting at the table for a brief review of her minutes.

"I've recorded everything, noting that next time you want to address sharing some of your admin duties. Is there anything else you'd like me to add to my notes?" she asked.

Mike walked over to the window, placing his hands in his pockets while staring out at the water.

"Were you expecting Keith to pay you a visit?" Mike asked.

Clara rose out of her seat.

"No, Mike. I swear I did not know he was coming. Wait... how do you know his name?" she asked.

"I met him when I walked over to the café to pick up the bagels. He sat next to me, listening to my conversation with Jonathan. Now I know why. He's pretty slick, if you ask me. I'm surprised you're into that type," he said.

"I'm not into him, Mike."

"Ha, you could've fooled me. Yesterday, you two were giving Solomons Island a full show, in broad daylight, for everyone to see. I found it to be rather interesting because here I've been trying to do the right thing, respecting your wishes, and waiting for just the right time to be with you. Man, was I foolish," he said.

"Mike, you have it all wrong. Keith is my-" Clara fell silent, feeling uncertain of how to proceed.

"He's not who you think he is. I mean-" She fumbled.

"Don't worry about it, Clara. I think you said it best in the beginning. Work relationships are great as long as things are going good. But, if things go south, then it can be awkward, right? Our best bet it to keep things strictly professional so it becomes no more awkward than it already is. I'll be out of here this week, so that should help. Is there anything else pertaining to the meeting that we need to discuss?" he asked while glancing at his watch.

Clara could feel the warm sensation of tears welling up in her eyes. She blinked to prevent them from falling and said, "No, I think we're done."

"Thanks, I'll be in my office if you need anything." Mike exited the conference room, leaving Clara sitting by herself.

CHAPTER 7

*B*ack at her desk, Clara called Dale, her lawyer. He was highly respected and had a proven record of handling many cases in the area. If Joan, her former boss, thought highly of him to handle her affairs, then Clara trusted he could help steer her in the right direction. Anything was better than sitting on the sidelines, waiting for Keith to show up again.

"Dale, this is Clara Covington calling. I'm at work right now, but if you're available to talk this afternoon, I could really use your advice. Please give me a call when you have a chance," she said in her message.

"Everything okay? You sound upset and you had little to say in our meeting, which is unusual for you," Mae said.

"I'm fine, Ms. Mae. Thanks for asking."

Mae checked the clipboard with all the schedules posted and continue talking to Clara.

"I understand. When something is troubling me, sometimes I find it hard to talk about it, too," she said.

Clara looked up at Mae but didn't say anything.

"This week hasn't exactly gotten off to a splendid start for me, either." She continued.

"Everything really is okay, but I'm sorry to hear you're not having a good week."

"Mmm hmm." She grunted.

Mae extended the blade on her box cutter and zipped it across the top of a delivery that arrived.

"You see, all the tell-tale signs that something is wrong shows up in the following ways for me. Weary eyes from lack of sleep, sometimes loss of appetite, and then there's my mood. Sometimes, I just get into a funk and I can't seem to shake it until my problem is solved. Talking about it may not be what you want to do, but I think it's healthy for you, Clara. So, what's bugging you? Did you and Mike hit a rough patch?"

Mae reached into the box and unpacked a new bulletin board.

"Nice. We could use one of these in the break room," Mae said.

"Yeah, I was thinking we needed a better space to post schedules and other work-related items," Clara said.

"So, tell me about it. What's eating away at you?" Mae asked.

"I guess I could ask you the same thing. I saw the way Jonathan passed you by this morning without saying so much as hello. What was that all about?"

"Ah, that. I guess that's what you call a bump in the road. Nothing that can't be fixed, I would imagine. I'm just not ready to deal with it," Mae replied.

"Interesting. Well, with my rough patch and your bump in the road, it sounds like we could both use a break," Clara said.

"So, you admit there's a patch?" Mae smiled.

"Yes, I admit it. But like yourself, it's nothing I care to talk about. Let's be honest here... half the office saw what happened yesterday, so even if I wanted to keep it a secret, I couldn't."

"Clara, if what we saw yesterday meant nothing to you, then let Mike know. I haven't known you for long, but even I could tell that wasn't your doing. Whoever that guy was, clearly showed up unannounced. Just explain your situation to Mike... he'll understand," Mae said.

"I tried to, but he didn't care to hear anything I had to say. If Mike doesn't want to take the time to hear me out, then I just have to move on. At this point I have bigger concerns so it's probably best that I focus on other things, anyway," Clara replied.

Mae stopped in the middle of breaking down the box and gave Clara a look out of the corner of her eye.

She walked over to the front side of the counter so she could see her face-to-face.

"Now, you listen here," she whispered.

"You two were made for each other. You are a perfect match and you'd be foolish not to do whatever you can to help him understand the truth. I knew from the moment I saw you two together it would someday lead to the perfect love story. Don't let whatever this brief hiccup is get in the way. Do you hear me?" Mae threatened.

Clara whispered in return.

"Is it that obvious that we have feelings for each other?" she asked.

"Ha! Is it obvious? The only ones who think it's still a secret are you and Mike. The rest of us are quite sick of the charade and are ready for you to go public with your feelings already."

Clara blew upward, causing her bangs to fall out of place.

"I need a mental health day... on the beach... with a glass of wine and my dog by my side," Clara said.

"That can be arranged. I don't have any tours this afternoon. I just came in to get some paperwork done. It's nothing I can't do while covering for you. Why don't you head home and take that well-deserved health day? Gather your thoughts and come up with your plan of action. I'll tell Mike you weren't feeling well and needed to go lie down." Mae offered.

"No, I feel guilty. I should probably stay."

"For what? Stay so you can continue to sulk all day? You know you won't be able to concentrate on anything. Go on... take the rest of the day. The job will be here when you get back, trust me." Mae encouraged Clara until she agreed and gave in.

Back at the house, her level of concern eased as soon as her feet hit the sand. The sound of the gentle ebb and flow of the water was just what she needed to melt her worries away. Unfortunately, the tranquility was short-lived when Dale's name appeared on her phone.

"Dale, how are you?" Clara answered.

"I'm well. It was a pleasant surprise to hear your message. How's everything going at the house?"

"It's great. Although, I often wonder how Joan spent all those years alone prior to taking me in as her housekeeper. This place is big enough to host a baseball team," she replied.

"Joan appreciated the finer things in life, including that beach house. But the key is she had a big heart."

"She sure did, Dale."

"So, how can I help you today? Your voice sounded a little rattled when I listened to the message. Is everything okay?"

"No, it's not okay. I'm in a bit of a bind and I need legal advice."

"What's up?" he asked.

"It's my ex. Actually, soon to be ex is a better way

to describe him. Somehow, my husband Keith received a notification letter about funds pertaining to the inheritance. He didn't know about the house until he got here, but he seemed to be well aware of how much I had in the bank. I was rather shocked, since all of my dealings were right here in your office in Maryland."

"That is surprising. Are you sure he doesn't have access to your account?" Dale asked.

"Not that I'm aware of. If he did, why wouldn't I have known about it long before now?"

"Take this the right way, but it's possible before now he wasn't nearly as interested in what was in your account. I'm certain your accounts look very different now that you have an inheritance," he said.

"Good point. I'll have to look into it. In the meantime, he's asking me for a good portion of the funds. He's claiming it's to make up for abandonment, which is a crock of you know what."

"Abandonment?" he asked.

"I didn't abandon him, Dale. I left him ten years ago because he was verbally and mentally abusive. It was not too long after my parents got into a terrible accident and I just couldn't take it anymore. He was constantly making comments about what I ate, how I dressed, and how a wife should behave. He judged me instead of loving me and ridiculed me whenever I made mistakes. I put up with it for a long time, but when the mind games began, I literally packed my bags and left. To this day, the only thing I regret is not making the divorce official immediately after," Clara said with tears of anger welling up in her eyes.

"Now, that piece of scum is asking me to make up for his years of so-called abandonment and suffering. He had the nerve to say he would take me to court. He said something about the state law that says once we've been married for seven years all of our assets would have to be split in the court of law."

"It sounds like he's putting his own twist on the law. How much is he asking you for?"

"Twenty-five percent. Dale, I swear if the courts take his side on this, I don't know what I'll do."

Clara paced around, leaving a pattern of footprints in the sand. Holly followed beside her, trying to keep up.

"I want you to take a deep breath. While I'm not a divorce lawyer, I feel pretty confident that this whole thing sounds fishy. Let me reach out to a good buddy of mine who can help answer a few questions and perhaps even represent you." He offered.

"Thanks, Dale."

"Not a problem. Clara, in the meantime, are you safe?" he asked.

"I think so. He showed up at the café and my job this week. But, I honestly believe he's trying to use the element of surprise as a scare tactic. He's all talk."

"I don't know, Clara. Showing up at your job is a bit much. What did he say?"

"He's looking for the money by tomorrow. What he doesn't know is if he shows up at my house or my job again-"

"Wait. Did you say he's been to your house as well?" Dale raised his tone.

"Yes."

"That's a threat to your safety and well-being," Dale responded.

"It's nothing I can't handle. He likes to play mind games, but he's not fooling anybody but himself. I'll pay top dollar to the lawyer who can make this go away for good," she said.

"You sound pretty confident that he won't pose a physical threat."

"I am, but I would like to get the papers filed for the divorce as soon as possible, and I need to receive some clear direction whether I'm obligated to share any funds with him."

"Of course. Let me make a few phone calls. If you don't hear from me this evening, I'll get back to you first thing in the morning." Dale promised.

"Thank you."

"You bet. Clara, what will you do if he comes looking for you tomorrow?"

"I'll dial 911 and see that he receives a one-way ticket to jail. As long as he doesn't step foot on my property or come to my job again, I have nothing to say. But, if he crosses the line, I'll call the police. It's that simple."

"Okay. Something tells me you should call them anyway, but I'll leave that up to you. Take care and I'll be in touch soon," he said.

~

Clara spent the rest of the day sitting on her lounge chair on the beach. A quiet lunch followed by a glass of wine was the perfect recipe to help relax her mind. She wanted so badly to call Mike and explain everything to him. If only he would listen. In some ways, she couldn't blame him. If she had been the one looking out the window at him, kissing another woman, she would choose to have nothing to do with him as well.

Amid Clara's daydreaming, Holly barked ferociously, which was her usual signal that someone was at the front door. She checked the cameras, feeling relieved that it was Mack.

"Hey, Mack. Give me a second. I'm heading toward the house now," Clara said through her phone, which was connected to the speakers on the camera.

"Are you trying to give me a heart attack with all your high-tech gadgets?" Mack responded.

"No, I just recently discovered the camera has a speaker component. Who knew?"

Clara dusted her feet off before entering the house.

"Yeah, but here's the thing. We're pretty peaceful

out here on the island. People leave their garage doors open during the day so the kids can run outside and play. All this high-tech gear is for city folks. It's been a long time since you've been a city girl, Clara. When are you going to get with the program?" she said, shouting into the speaker.

Clara opened the front door, causing Mack to jump.

"Maybe never. I see nothing wrong with having a little extra security."

She invited Mack in, locked the door, and rescued Mack from Holly's playful yapping.

"Ms. Mae stopped by the café to pick up lunch. She told me you were feeling kind of under the weather, so I thought I'd come by and check on you... and by under the weather I detected she meant something was weighing on your heart more than anything else."

Clara wiped away an immediate windfall of tears. The frustration was taking its toll. It seemed as if everyone else around her always had it together. Her life used to be that simple, boring, even mundane. But she was thinking the series of events following her boss' death, including inheriting her money, was a curse that caused more trouble than not.

"Clara, talk to me. Does this have anything to do with your ex?" Mackenzie asked.

Clara nodded.

"Come sit down with me. Let's talk about it."

In the kitchen Clara poured a glass for the two of them and placed an assortment of snacks out.

"Where do I begin? It honestly feels like I'm trapped in the middle of a bad dream...I want to wake up from the dream, but I can't."

"What happened?" Mack continued to press.

"The jerk you saw at the café is my husband, as I explained to you before. Our relationship was... toxic to say the least. He never spoke words that would build me up, only words that would tear me down. He played manipulative mind games that made me question my actions and my values. Nothing was ever good enough with him. Nothing. Not long after my parents' accident, you'd think he'd be more empa-thetic, more loving, more compassionate. No, not him. He didn't know how. Instead, he got worse and in all honesty, I couldn't take it anymore. I left him." Clara explained.

"Good! Good for you, Clara. You deserve so much better."

"I agree. The only problem is, I never filed for an official divorce. And, now, several years later, somehow the creep gets wind of the fact that I have a little money and now he wants to claim abandon-ment. He's expecting me to share a large portion of the inheritance, and if I don't, he's threatening to take me to court."

"No, ma'am. That's not how it works where I

come from. Did you get yourself a lawyer?" Mack asked.

"I called Dale. He's looking into it now and is supposed to get back to me."

"I know it's easier said than done, but try not to worry. He'll help you. I know he will. What did Mike have to say about all this?" she asked.

"Ha! Not much after he saw us kissing the other day," Clara said sarcastically.

"Wait. What?"

"Yep, the creep stopped by my job. We stepped outside to talk so I wouldn't share all my business with everybody. He took advantage of the situation and pulled me toward him for a kiss. I swear he did it because he saw he had an audience looking through the window."

"Nooo," Mack replied.

"Yes! Mike was pissed. He's said very little to me since then. I tried to talk to him twice, but he won't hear me out. The irony of it all is he's leaving this week to start his new schedule at the North Beach location. Do you know how much we've been waiting for this opportunity? Mike working at the other location was our freedom ticket to pursuing a normal relationship with each other. I miss him, Mack. But no matter what I do, he doesn't want to talk to me. It's just like I said... this is all one big nightmare, and I can't seem to wake up to save my life."

"Clara, let's be reasonable here. Mike is head over

heels about you. He smiles from ear to ear at the mention of your name. That can't just go away overnight. His feelings are hurt, that's all. Don't give up. Call him. Show up at his place... do whatever you have to. I'll set him straight the next time he comes in the café if you want me to," Mack said.

"No. Please don't. The last thing I need is for all of Solomons Island to hear about this over a brisket sandwich at the café."

"Sounds funny, now that you put it like that." Mack chuckled.

"Yeah, well, trust me, there is nothing funny about this. Keith... my soon to be ex-husband, has gone as far as leaving a note on my doorstep, tracking me down at the café, and showing up at my job. I need to send a clear message to him before I can focus on getting through to Mike."

"Good grief! I didn't realize he'd done all that. Even though I sensed something was strange about him from the first day he came into the café. You need to have the nut job arrested."

"For what? Leaving a note at my door or telling me, as my husband, that I should share my inheritance with him? I may not like it, but in the eyes of the court, has he really committed a crime?" Clara asked.

"You sound like you're defending him."

"I'm not defending him. I'm just trying to be realistic," Clara replied.

"I don't know how the courts would view this, but he needs to be dealt with before it gets any further out of hand." Mack argued.

"I know. Look, I left work early today so I could gather my thoughts and come up with some sort of plan-"

"Say no more. I'm sorry, Clara. The last thing you need is me getting you all riled up. I really stopped by just to check on you and entice you to indulge in a piece of your favorite cake from the café."

Mack pulled out a thick slice of cheesecake from her purse, wrapped in saran wrap, and moved it around Clara's nose. All the tension melted off at the sight of her friend's kind gesture.

CHAPTER 8

"Good morning, Clara," Savannah said in a melodious voice.

She slipped in the front door, giving off a lingering scent of vanilla mist. She wore her hair up in a bun, had a gorgeous tan, and enough cleavage to distract every man on the island.

"Savannah, how can I help you today?" Clara responded.

"I'm here to see Mike. He's expecting me."

"Really?" she asked.

Savannah popped her chewing gum and nodded.

"All right, well, I'll check to see if he's available," she said.

"Ah, don't bother. I'll just head to his office. We just got off the phone. He knows I'm coming." Savannah smirked and walked past Clara to the back of the store.

Clara raised the corner of her mouth, trying to put together a smile. She wasn't sure how successful she was at it, and a part of her didn't care. She thought it was pretty low of Mike to dangle Savannah in front of her like an ornament on a tree. But at this point, everything was fair game given that she had publicly kissed a guy in front of his face.

"Clara, Clara, Clara... how are you today?" Jonathan said while emerging from the back.

"I've had better days. How are you doing?" she asked.

"I'm well, thank you."

He walked around to the front counter. At first, he adjusted a few of the brochures, and then he rested on the front counter to talk.

"You know what you need, don't you?" he asked.

Clara raised her eyes while still holding her fingers on the keyboard of her computer.

"No, Jonathan. Tell me. What do I need?"

He leaned closer, pointed his finger at her, and said, "You need to stop making room for someone else to steal him away from you. Tell him how you feel and claim what's yours," he said.

"For the love of God. Not you, too." Clara massaged her temples.

"What do you mean, not me, too?"

"Well, hmm, let's see. Where do I begin? First,

it's Ms. Mae, and now you. You two have all the advice in the world for me but can't seem to get your own act together to save your life," Clara said.

"Is that what she told you?"

"Noo," she said with guilt in her voice.

"That's just what I gathered from the way you two haven't been speaking to each other. It's not the way you normally behave. I'm sorry. I shouldn't have snapped at you like that." She confessed.

"It's just... I have a lot on my plate right now, so ideally claiming what's mine would make sense, but he's not mine. He never was. Plus, it's complicated. It's better for me to leave relationship matters alone and stay focused on work," she said.

Jonathan tapped on the counter.

"Look, I'm not one to normally get involved, but I'm trying to save you from yourself."

"Pardon me?" she asked.

"That's right. I'm trying to save you from making the same mistake that Mae and I are making right now. I recognize it just as plain as day. Mae holds a lot of her feelings inside. She keeps everything locked up and tucked away in her secret vault of thoughts. I, on the other hand, put up a wall to protect my feelings, but that doesn't make it right. This kind of behavior has gotten us nowhere. Don't be like us. Going around and pretending solves absolutely nothing. In actuality, it only makes thing worse. When Savannah leaves... you need to talk to him. Communicate with him, Clara. Us men can be stubborn. Help him see the way." Jonathan begged.

"If only it were that easy," she responded.

"It is that easy. I don't care about whatever else is going on in your life. It will iron itself out. Do something before it's too late."

"Will you follow your own advice?" Clara asked.

"Ha! I'll work on it. It takes two to tango, you know."

"My point exactly. I'll tell you one thing... I wish his little guest would tango on out of here." She smiled but meant every word.

"Meh, I wouldn't sweat it. There's nothing there. Mike doesn't care for Savannah the way he cares for you. If you tell him I said it, I'll deny it all day." Jonathan warned and then exited to the back again.

"Clara, good to see you. I'm glad you could join me for a lunch appointment." Dale stood to greet her.

"Thanks for having me."

"I'd like you to meet Kolton, one of my best friends and a fantastic divorce attorney, if I might add. We've known each other since college."

Kolton stood from his seat and extended his hand to Clara.

"Nice to meet you, Ms. Covington."

"Likewise. Please, call me Clara."

"All right, Clara."

"I explained the urgency of the situation, and Kolton carved out some time to meet with us today." Dale explained.

"You don't know how much I appreciate this. When I received the message from Dale, that you were available, I was so relieved. The sooner I can get Keith out of my life, the better," she said.

"Yes, Dale shared your story with me. I'd love to hear it from your perspective... maybe just highlighting the events that brought us to where we are today," Kolton replied.

"Oh, it's pretty simple. Money has brought us to this point. Apparently, Keith will do whatever it takes to get his hands on it. If I had to guess, maybe he's down on his luck. Maybe it's been this way for a while. Who knows. The only thing I still can't seem to figure out is how he knows about the money. We haven't been in touch with each other in years."

"Do you still have any shared accounts?" Kolton asked.

"No. At one point both of our names were on everything, but I thought I went through the proper channels to remove his name once I moved. There really shouldn't be an issue there," Clara said.

"Sometimes you'd be surprised to know what people are capable of. Maybe that's something we need to help you look into. The one thing I hope to do is put your mind at ease. I can't think of one judge who would approve of him receiving a share of your inheritance. An inheritance is not considered marital property; therefore, he doesn't have a leg to stand on," he said.

Clara slinked back in her chair and closed her eyes for a moment.

"Ms. Covington, the only thing you need to be concerned about is how quickly we can get these divorce papers processed. From what I can see, even that shouldn't be an issue for you."

"Clara." She breathed a sigh of relief while stating her own name.

"I'm sorry?" he asked.

"Please, call me Clara. You just don't know how good it feels to hear you utter those words. Keith sounded so confident, like he knew what he was saying, and I like an idiot believed it was true."

"Well, let me be the first to tell you otherwise. How about we start with some basic information? I have a few forms for you to fill out regarding our agreement should you decide to hire me as your lawyer. Then, I'll need some information about Keith as well." Kolton explained.

"Yes, sir. I'll fill out whatever it takes. There's one more thing that comes to mind," she said.

"Sure. How can I help?" Kolton asked.

"Keith told me he wanted the money today. I think he's preparing to leave town. I know nothing about where he's staying, and he wasn't even clear with me about where and how he wanted to carry this out. But, I know him, and he will show up as promised. It's only a matter of time."

"You can file a complaint against him if you feel threatened. If he persists, you can even get a restraining order," Kolton replied.

Clara looked over at Dale.

"Oh, man. Doesn't this sound familiar. A few months back, I had to have a similar conversation regarding Joan's niece and her brother. Now look. Sometimes I really question whether or not this inheritance was a blessing or a curse," Clara said.

Kolton looked at Dale with a confused expression.

"Joan left her niece and other family members out of the will. She gave everything to Clara, and let's just say, they didn't take too kindly to the idea." Dale explained.

"Ah, I see. Yeah, unfortunately, money can cause people to act ugly, but know that the law is on your side. All the odds are stacked in your favor, and again, if you think you're being threatened, we can do something about that as well," he said.

"I consider myself to be a pretty excellent judge of character. It's been a while, but I know what makes Keith tick and how far he's willing to push things. I think I'll be just fine."

"Well, here's my business card with my cell

number included. Let me know if you change your mind." Kolton offered.

"I will."

"In the meantime, we should follow up with another appointment. Give me a couple of days to do some digging and round up any additional necessary paperwork. You have my information if you need me before then. If not, you'll hear from me no later than the beginning of next week," he said.

"Kolton, I can't thank you enough," Clara said while shaking his hand.

"It's my pleasure."

"And Dale, I really appreciate you making the connection for me. I know I always say I'll pop my head in and say hi every once in a while. Perhaps next time I really can stop by just to say hello, minus all the drama." Clara gave Dale a hug. He was the only person left who had a close relationship and love for her boss, Joan.

Clara pulled her old Honda up to the storefront of Lighthouse Tours, right behind Mike's jeep. She turned the engine off and rested her head back with ten minutes to spare on her lunch break. She could smell the scent of grilled food from the café while feeling the gentle June breeze blow strands of hair across her face. In the background, she could hear what sounded like buoy bells in the distance. A knocking sound on her trunk interrupted the tranquility.

"Wake up, sleepyhead." Josh teased.

"Josh, you scared the daylights out of me. Do it again and see what happens." Clara threatened.

"Yikes, just having a little fun with you, that's all. I saw you pull into the space and I figured since I was out here taking a smoking break, I'd come over and say hello," he said.

"Mmm hmm. You ought to know better than to walk up on somebody like that. And since when did you take up smoking?"

"Since Uncle Sam started collecting over thirty percent of the profits from my part-time auto parts business. Around tax time to be exact. Although, I probably started dabbling around with cigarettes a little before then to be honest. Want to try one?" he asked.

"Me? No, I'll leave that up to you. The one time I tried a cigarette in high school I nearly coughed up a lung." Clara rolled up her windows and stepped out of the car.

"So, I take it business is going well, if you owe taxes."

"It's not doing too badly. I just need more time in the day to get things done. Serving tables at the café pays me decent and all... but the real money is in ownership," Josh replied.

"So they say. Just be careful. Sometimes having more money isn't always a good thing."

"Yeah, well, let me be the judge of that. I think I'd manage just fine," he said.

Clara responded with a half-surprised laugh.

"Hey, my lunch break is just about over, so I better get inside. Really quick, I was wondering if you've seen a guy wearing a baseball cap today? He's from out of town... usually sits at a window seat," she said.

"Oh, yeah, I know who you're speaking about. Mack told me about him and asked me to keep an eye out. I haven't seen him in the last couple of days. Is everything all right? You know we have your back if needed."

"Thanks, Josh. Everything's going to be fine. Just let me know if you see him, okay? His name is Keith... Keith Brown," she replied.

"Will do." Josh tipped his hat off to her and waved as Clara disappeared into Lighthouse Tours.

She slipped her purse away and then walked to Mike's office door. Feeling hesitant at first, Clara checked around for the other staff members, hoping things would stay quiet. She pressed her ear against the door to make sure he didn't sound occupied, and then knocked gently and waited for a response.

"Come in," Mike said.

She fixed her hair, wiped the lining of her lips, and walked in.

"Hey, Mike. Do you have a free moment?" she asked.

"Uh, my plate is rather full. I have tons to sort through before heading over to the other store in about an hour. Is it urgent?"

It didn't get past Clara that he didn't look up the entire time he was speaking.

Come on, girl. You got this, she thought.

"Well, if by urgent, you mean it's a work-related matter that can't wait... not really. But, I definitely think it's something you need to hear."

"Clara, we've been over this already. It's fine, really. You don't have to-"

"I know I don't have to, Mike, but since you haven't given me the chance to explain, then I'm making one last ditch effort... right here... and right now. Are you going to stop ignoring me and listen to what I have to say or not?" She demanded.

He put his pen down and sat back in his chair.

"All right. It seems as if I don't have much of a choice. The floor is yours," he replied.

Clara didn't know whether to be agitated at his tone and simply forget about it or if she should set the record straight. The one thing that was clear... he definitely had the wrong idea about her.

"I'm not one for going around proving my character, my innocence, or lack thereof to anybody. I'm a good person and would never do anything out of spite or to be hurtful. What you saw the other day is what Keith wanted you to see. An act... a show that he put on for his audience with no substance behind it," she said.

He sat in complete silence, so she continued.

"Keith is my soon to be ex-husband. I left him ten years ago, when I moved out here to flee an abusive marriage."

"I thought you told me you needed a change after your parents' accident," he said.

"I did. My life was in absolute shambles. Everything was falling apart. I lost my parents, my relationship with my sister was at the tipping point, and Keith tried to play every manipulative mind game he could to keep me under his control. All of that was enough to make me flee New York, never to return again. But, did you really expect me to lay it all on the line as we're still getting to know each other? That's a bit much, don't you think?" she asked.

"So, if you left him, why is he here now?" Mike asked.

"He's here for one thing... money! What do they say about money? I think they call it the root of all evil. It can draw in the worst of them. Keith found out about my inheritance, and now he thinks I'm supposed to share some of it with him. He's going as far as threatening to take me to court if I don't give up twenty-five percent." Clara explained.

"I'm sorry. I didn't know," he said, seeming concerned.

"Exactly. You just assumed, Mike. Whatever happened to giving me the benefit of the doubt? Do you really think I would stand across the street from your business in the middle of the day and kiss another man? Come on, you have to know me better than that," she said.

Mike stood to approach her.

"Wait. Let me finish telling you everything so you know who you're dealing with. This may have changed our personal relationship, but you should at least know who I am as your employee." She explained.

"Clara, I-"

"Let me finish. I made the worst mistake in the world by leaving him without making the divorce official. All I wanted to do was run and get as far out of his sight as possible. I didn't want to have contact with him, and I didn't even want to utter his name. I probably still wouldn't mention his name if he hadn't showed up like this. But, I guess sometimes things happen for the better. I've already met with a lawyer, and I'm going to do everything within my power to bring this to an end once and for all. If you're concerned about him coming around here or me bringing any other personal matters to the office, it shouldn't be an issue much longer." She paused.

Mike waited and then carefully approached the other side of the desk.

"May I speak now?" he asked.

"Sure."

"I'm sorry. I was a complete jerk for not hearing you out. From where I stood it just looked like... ugh. I don't know. I thought things were going well with us, so when I saw you two together-"

"It made you jealous?" she asked.

"Well, yeah." He lowered his voice.

"Look, I get it. The whole thing looks bad. I'm not asking you to justify your reaction, but I am asking you to trust my character, that's all," she said.

They remained in awkward silence. Clara could hear her heart thumping and hoped Mike couldn't hear it. She could smell the fresh scent of his cologne and wished he would grab her and hold her as he had a few days earlier. When neither of them moved, she reached for the doorknob instead.

"You should get back to work. I don't want to hold you up. I know you have a lot coming up in the next few days. Thank you for taking the time to hear me out," she said.

Mike began to speak, but by then the door was already open with Ms. Mae standing on the other side.

CHAPTER 9

A blue Ford Bronco with a New York license plate sat idle and parked backwards in front of Clara's garage door. Typically, she'd pull in, letting the door down behind her. Instead, she parked head on, blocking the car in, while observing the man with a rustic baseball cap, who was undoubtedly Keith.

She shut the engine off and exited the car, ready to confront him face to face.

"Hello there, honey. How was your day?" Keith said as he got out of the Bronco.

"Cut the small talk, Keith. I haven't been your honey for a long time."

"Whoa, now. Hold on there. I know it's been a while, but true love stands the test of time," he said.

"Is that what you call it? True love?" she asked.

"That's what I'll call it before the judge, if necessary."

"Interesting," Clara responded.

"It was pretty bold of you to show up here at the house again. Although, I can't say I wasn't expecting you. You were always pretty predictable," she said.

"Is that so? Well, that's a good thing, I suppose. If you were expecting me, then I'm sure you're prepared to hand over my share of the money."

"About that. While you have all these well thought out plans for what you would tell a judge in court, I've been making plans of my own. I've listened to everything you had to say and weighed all my options. I think I'll pass on your offer. The only thing I'll be giving you are the official divorce papers that I should've served you a long time ago," she said with a look of disdain.

"Clara, something tells me you're not thinking this through."

"There's nothing to think about, Keith. I'm just sorry you drove all the way out here and wasted your time. Did you really think I would just give in to such a ridiculous request? I don't owe you anything."

Keith leaned on the front bumper of his truck and tugged Clara by her belt toward him. She slapped his hand down.

"I'm not the same woman you knew back then. I will make you wish you never set foot on Solomons Island. If you want to go toe to toe with me in court, then let's go. I've already hired a lawyer. I will chew you up and then spit you out if you even dare think about messing with me." She threatened.

"Darlin, since when did you become so hostile toward me?" he asked.

Clara pointed her finger at him, standing so close she nearly jabbed him in the chest.

"Long before the day I left your sorry behind. Let me be very clear with you, Keith. I'm not playing any silly games with you. You call yourself showing up, hanging around all the local spots and making a public spectacle out of me in this town. But, you weren't thinking, and as a result, everybody knows you by name. They can identify what you look like and they all know your motive for being here. So, if I were you, I would get back in your truck and go crawl back under whatever rock you've been living under for ten years. If you don't, I'm going to take my lawyer up on his idea to call the police and report you. Do I make myself clear?"

Keith straightened up, removed his keys out of his pocket, and proceeded to return to the truck.

"Well, you don't have to tell me twice. It's obvious I'm not welcomed here, so I guess I'll see you in court," he said.

"I highly doubt it," Clara replied.

She stood with hands on her hip, watching him close the door. Clara was so agitated, he had to gesture for her to move her car out of the way.

"Gladly," she shouted, with tears of relief welling up in her eyes.

The engine to Mike's jeep came roaring up the driveway.

He honked the horn.

"Clara, you all right?" Mike yelled.

"I'm fine." She quickly wiped her eyes. "I'll be even better as soon as I back out and let the loser be on his way," she said, looking like she could spit at the idea of Keith's existence.

"Do you need me to deal with him?" Mike said as he glanced over at the Bronco.

"I think he received my message loud and clear. Although, I'm sure your presence doesn't hurt," she said.

"Anything for you," he responded.

Keith laid on the horn a few times.

"Come on, already. I don't have all day," he shouted.

"Hey, show some respect, man. She's coming." Mike fired back and pulled his jeep out of the way.

Inside the house Clara broke down in tears.

"Come here," Mike said.

She collapsed in his arms, allowing the tears to flow.

"You've had it pretty rough, kiddo. But, I promise

from here on out, this will be the end of it," Mike said.

"What do you mean?"

He pulled her chin up so their eyes could meet.

"I promise if you let me love you, the way you deserve to be loved, your days of turmoil will be a thing of the past. Clara, all I've ever wanted since we first met was to be with you and freely love you. I can take care of you and protect you from that idiot or anybody else who ever tries to cross you again. You have to believe me. I want to be here for you." He traced her eyebrows and then her cheeks with his gentle touch.

"What about Savannah?" she asked.

"When word got to her that I was leaving to spend time at the new store, she tried to pay me one last visit. Her efforts weren't successful, Clara. It's you that I want," he responded.

"She's pretty bold. She told me you were expecting her."

"Yep, that sounds like something she would do. And here I was thinking maybe you stepped away from the front desk, making it easy for her to come to my office door." Mike laughed

She pulled Mike close with both hands and consumed his lips with hers. They indulged each other for a while without interruption before pausing.

"Say it again," she whispered.

"Which part?"

"The promise," she said.

"I promise if you let me love you the way you deserve to be loved, your days of turmoil will be a thing of the past. I mean it, Clara. So help me I do."

"I know you do you."

"Do you recall the evening I camped out in your living room when you were living back at the apartment?" he asked.

"How could I forget? If you hadn't stayed with me that night, I probably would've barricaded myself in, never to come out again," she said lightheartedly.

"Yeah, well, I wanted the role of being your protector that night, and it still hasn't changed today."

That's so sweet, Mike."

"Thank you, but I don't want to be sweet. I want to be your man."

She drew in a breath while he wiped her tear-stained skin.

"Withholding ourselves from one another the way we have for the sake of being professional was good while it lasted. But, I want you in my life, and I'm not ashamed to admit it to the whole world... starting with Solomons Island," he said.

She giggled like a young girl in love.

"All of Solomons Island?" she asked while tugging on his shirt.

"Plus the whole world...don't forget that part."

She was ready to take things to the next level, feeling completely in sync with Mike, desiring to be

with him. If he could turn a blind eye to the tumul-
tuous roller coaster her life had been since they met,
she knew he was worth keeping around.

"Holly has been hovering by your back door for a
while now. You think she needs to go outside?" he
asked.

"Probably. I'll open the door. Lately, she's been
pretty good about going out on her own. Want to
walk down to the beach with me?" she asked.

"Sure."

Holly took off, finding her usual spot to take care
of business. Clara walked barefooted through the
backyard and down to the sand, leading Mike by the
finger.

"I'd like to introduce you to my favorite place.
My getaway, if you will."

She lifted her hands and twirled, taking in the
evening breeze.

"This is my happy place. When I worked for
Joan, I used to wait until after hours to come out here
and relax and clear my mind. Who would've ever
thought back then this place would become my own
someday?" she said while drawing a few lines in the
sand with her toes.

"I can see why it's your happy place. This is
breathtaking," he said.

"Thank you, I try to get out here as often as I can
to mentally sort things out. Lately, I've been thinking
things were really on track, until Keith showed up."

He put his hand out and stopped her from walking any further.

"Clara, your life is on track. This was an unforeseeable hiccup that will eventually go away once he's served those papers. You have to believe that things are looking up. If Joan were still alive, I bet she'd say the same."

"You're right. If she were still alive, she would've been thrilled to meet you. All she ever wanted was to see me settle down with someone who would make me happy."

Holly came galloping through the sand at full speed, wagging her tail and happy to join them for a walk.

"Good girl, Holly."

Mike pet Holly, then found a place to sit, inviting Clara to join him.

"I feel pretty confident that her wish will come true. The question that remains unanswered is how do you feel about it?" he asked.

"Do you want full transparency?"

"Always," he said.

"All right, then, I'm going to lay it all on the line. I think it couldn't be more obvious how I feel about you, Mike. When you do things like create so-called outings for job training, which are really nothing but secret dates, I'm there, all the way, loving every minute of it. When you sneak into the supply room to pull me close and kiss me, again, I'm all in-"

"That's a lie and you know it. You totally fuss at me for doing that and remind me of how unprofessional it is." He teased.

She nudged him on the arm.

"That's because it is unprofessional. Hey, I'm trying to help make the business look good, okay." She laughed.

He kissed the top of her hand. "Continue, please. I want to hear more."

"You gave me a chance to work at Lighthouse Tours when I was down on my luck and desperate. All this came after I got into a car accident with you. Most people would've been done after that, but not you. Then, you stood by my side through all the drama with inheriting this place and continued drama as I now deal with Keith. Even though my life has changed, you don't see me for what I have, you see me for who I am. How can I resist a man like that?" She ruffled his hair to lighten things up. It was her way of pressing through the vulnerability, which hadn't always been easy for her.

"Yeah, I guess it's been kind of crazy the way things came together. But, when it's right, it's right."

"Agreed."

They cuddled with playful Holly and listened to the tranquil waves for a while.

"Hey, Mike. You're supposed to be heading over to the new office this afternoon. What happened?

How did you make your way over to my house instead?"

"I'll head over there in the morning. There was no way I could let our conversation end the way it did. I wouldn't be able to focus until we had a chance to talk." He admitted.

"I see. Well, there is something you could focus on now." She snuggled up closer, feeling happy and safe having him there by her side.

~

The next day Clara stopped by the café for an evening meal and to catch up with her old friend. She crossed the threshold and was greeted by the familiar sound of the after five o'clock hustle and bustle.

"Well, look who just walked in. Clara Covington, we've missed you. I can't recall the last time I saw you walking through the doors of the café. Come on over here and make yourself comfortable." Mack pointed toward a seat at the front counter.

"It hasn't been that long, has it?" she asked.

"Maybe a week or so, but it feels like an eternity. You know the place is not the same without you."

"Aww, Mack, you're sweet, but I'm sure you can understand why I had to take a few days off. Speaking of which, have you seen him around to-day?" She wondered if Keith finally took the hint to leave.

"No, I was hoping I wouldn't see him ever again," Mackenzie responded.

"That makes two of us. I had a talk with him yesterday that hopefully set him straight. He also had a chance to see Mike. It was unplanned but there's nothing like having a male presence around to help send a message."

"I hear ya, hun. I just want this thing to be over with so you and Mike can get on with your lives."

"Me, too. Dale introduced me to a divorce lawyer. A guy by the name of Kolton Maxwell," she said.

"Oh, yeah, Kolton. I've heard he's one of the best. Never met him or anything but a few of the locals have mentioned his name before."

Mackenzie was interrupted by Mrs. Dudley who was sitting in the corner flailing her arms around, trying to get her attention.

"Oh, good Lord. Clara, I'll be right back. Mrs. Dudley is up to her usual. I'll bet even after reviewing the whole menu, which she knows by heart, she's going to try and ask me for the Monday night special, even though it's Thursday. Can I bring you a drink on the way back?" she asked.

"I'll take a coke. If you can, please put in an order of crab cakes with fries, for me."

"Will do. I'll be right back.

Clara skimmed the crowd, observing the bridge club in full swing with one of the players announcing *"ace high,"* and the other trying to get a quick peek at her cards. The front counter was packed with mostly single guys from the neighborhood who'd rather eat at the café than cook for themselves at home.

"Hey, Clara. Long time no see." Chloe approached the counter pulling her tablet out of her apron.

"Chloe, it's so good to see you. How are you? How's everything going with school?"

"I just graduated," she said.

"Stop! Man, did time fly or what?"

"I know. I wrote tons of papers, read a ton of books, perfected a million recipes, and now I can officially say that I have a degree in culinary arts," Chloe responded.

"Wow, so what's your next plan? Off to grad school in the fall?"

"Not quite. My folks and I decided it might be smart to take a year off to give us a little breathing room, financially. I plan on building up my resume and after the year is up, grad school here I come." Chloe smiled.

"That's wonderful. I'm happy for you, Chloe. You oughta go back there and show Chef a thing or two." Clara leaned over and whispered, "He's been slipping on the hot open turkey sandwiches lately."

Chloe laughed at the comment and promised to look for opportunities to gain more experience in the back kitchen whenever Chef would allow it.

Mack returned and slipped a piece of paper in Chloe's hand.

"Chloe, can you do me a favor and put this order in with Chef? I'm going to take my fifteen-minute break and steal Clara for that amount of time to take a little evening walk. By the time we get back, it should be hot and ready for her, okay?" she said.

"Yes, ma'am."

"Oh, and I told Josh already. He's looking after the bridge club and Mrs. Dudley's whole section. Just make sure you come back out and help him if he needs it." Mackenzie requested.

"I'm on it."

Mackenzie turned to Clara. "Why don't you leave that menu on your seat as a place holder. Let's go get some fresh air until your meal is ready," she said.

"Sure, I could use a little girl time."

"Don't worry, I have you covered." Mack patted her on the back.

Outside, they began strolling down the tree lined sidewalk across the street from the dock.

"Talk to me, Clara. I can't imagine what these last few days have been like for you. It seems like you can't catch a break," Mackenzie said.

"It's definitely been an interesting time. I probably was the laughing stock of the town after that whole charade with Keith."

"Says who? Solomons Island has your back. We

were all keeping an eye out for the creep. He's lucky he didn't return again is the only thing I can say." Mack emphasized with sass.

"Really?"

"Clara, yes. I don't know where you think you are, but we look out for each other out here. Even if Solomons didn't have your back, I do. I'm your friend and I'm concerned about you. If you ever have something this serious going on in your life, please know that you can come to me without judgement." Mack paused.

"That means the world to me. I don't know why I held this in so long. Keith was just a terrible memory that I wanted to erase from my memory bank. I swear I'm not holding anything else back. He was my deepest and darkest skeleton, and now the cat is completely out of the bag," Clara said.

"Oh, honey, we all have skeletons. Anybody who tries to convince you otherwise is playing you for a fool."

"Yeah, but my skeleton was pretty bad."

"Eh eh. Don't do that to yourself." Mack cautioned.

"Do what?"

"Hold yourself to the fire like that. You're human and to be quite frank, I don't blame you for handling this the way you did. Heck, I didn't even know the guy but if I did, I'd be looking to get away from him and erase the past just as quickly. It's called being normal." Mack was like a wise old soul trapped in a fifty-year-old body, always offering the most comforting and level-headed advice.

"You know what? You're right. To mark this occasion of renewed thinking, I'm making today the start of my brand new life. This morning I kept thinking about how I can't wait until Kolton gets me out of this mess. But, in some ways, that's like giving Keith the power to have a hold on me mentally until the divorce papers are served. That's no way to live. I'm not going to let fear win, and I'm certainly not going to blame myself for something I did or didn't do."

The silhouette of a couple standing hand- in- hand by the dock made Clara take notice and smile. Even in the midst of turmoil her heart was hopeful and longing for her fresh start to begin with Mike.

"I'm sure I don't have to tell you this, but love can be beautiful, Clara. I hope this experience won't cause you to retreat from your opportunity at love with Mike," Mack said in a curious tone.

"I'm determined not to let this get in the way. Last night he came by to talk things over with me. He actually showed up just in the nick of time. Keith was waiting in my driveway when I got home," she said.

"No way."

"Yep, but that's all over with now. It's like I said earlier...I definitely set him straight and let him know I wasn't buying into his threats. I'm certain now that he's seen for himself that I've moved on, Keith won't be bothering me, anymore. But to be sure, I told him if he does, I would call the police."

"Good," Mack said, stopping in front of a nearby hair salon.

"So, where does this leave you and Mike? Last time we talked he didn't listen to anything you had to say. What changed his mind?"

A smiled emerged on Clara's face.

"I marched right into his office...well, it was more like I knocked on his door and waited for an invite... either way, I told him a thing or two as well," she said.

Mack clapped her hands and laughed loud enough for the couple across the street to hear her.

"That's my girl. What did you say to him?"

"I told him the truth about what happened. I told him that Keith just wanted an audience and that's why he did what he did. I mean, come on, Mack. Do I seem like the type that would do something like that?" Clara asked.

"You would if it was Mike!" She bursted into another round of laughter.

"Perhaps. But, you get my point, and thankfully, he did, too. We kind of ended things in a weird place at first, but by the end of the evening, he came over to apologize and express his love for me." She smiled.

"Ooh, his love? Clara what did you do to that man?"

"I didn't do anything besides ask him to wait a while," she said.

"There's your secret sauce, right there. He's probably been dreaming about you day and night."

"Mack, you're ridiculous."

"Well, ridiculous or not, you know that I'm right. He's a good man, Clara. I've told you that plenty of times before. You better quit playing around and claim him for yourself. Now, my break is just about over. Come on back to the café with me so you can eat and so you can meet my new beau. He's stopping by in a half hour." Mack smiled, revealing her pearly whites at the mere mention of her new guy, Bill.

CHAPTER 10

The guests on Mae's boat tour disembarked, promising to return soon. It was a jovial group of housewives visiting the island on a weekend getaway. They spent the entire tour admiring the sites, sipping their beverages of choice, and gossiping with one another.

Back at the dock, Jonathan was waiting for her arrival.

"This is your last tour for the day, right?" he said as he approached her.

"Well, hello to you, too. So nice to see that you're talking to me again." Mae grumbled.

She gave him the once over before relaxing her tough girl stance.

"Yes, it's my last tour." She confessed.

"Good. Come with me." Jonathan turned to leave just as fast as he'd approached her.

Mae's eyebrows were drawn as she stood in confusion.

"Aren't you going to ask me if I want to join you?" she said.

"No, I'm not. If you want to miss what's about to happen, it will be your loss, not mine." He barked back and disappeared into the building.

In the office, Mae notified Clara that she'd return in a little while. She motioned her eyes toward Jonathan's back, signaling that he was up to something.

Clara crossed her fingers, but Mae knew it was going to take way more than good luck and finger crossing to figure Jonathan out.

Outside, he left the passenger door to his pickup truck opened for her and went around to hop in the driver's seat.

She got in on the passenger's side and shut the door. "Jonathan, where are we going?"

"Do you trust me?" he asked.

"You know I do, but I still have the right to know. Who's to say I didn't have some important paperwork to fill out back at the office?"

"It will be there when you get back," he replied.

"You know, sometimes I don't know what to make of your behavior. I really don't. Things were fine with us. Then, we have one conversation that didn't go the way you wanted and you storm off. We haven't talked in well over a week, and now this. What has gotten into you?" she asked.

"Mae, now is not the time. We'll be where we're going in less than five minutes. Just enjoy the ride."

She grunted, folding her arms in disgust. She didn't think it was okay that he was in charge of when they spoke and when they didn't. But, since she was already in the car with him, she figured it was best to just go along with it.

They turned down an access road, which led to the entrance of a small beach. During midafternoon you could count on a few stray visitors and tons of tranquility, while watching the boats pass by.

"Oh, for heaven's sake. Jonathan, what in the world-"

"Mae. Stop making this so difficult and come with me, please?" he asked.

She bit her lip and hopped out of the truck.

"I suppose you want me to ruin my new shoes, too. No questions asked. Just walk through the sand and be quiet, Mae." She spoke loud enough for Jonathan to hear her but was really just babbling to herself.

Jonathan walked a few feet ahead of her toward the water and stopped.

"No, Mae. I don't want you to ruin your new shoes. I don't want you to do anything you don't want to do. You can turn around and get back in the truck, if you really don't want to be here. But, you should at least know why we're here first," he said, sounding stern.

"Well, that's all I wanted to know to begin with."

Jonathan closed his eyes and took a deep breath.

"Woman, why are you making this so difficult?" He reached in his pocket and took out a light blue box. With a quick tug at his pant leg, he bent down on his knee and opened the box.

"Mae, I brought you here for two reasons. Number one, we met by the water. It's where our friendship began well over eight years ago. Now, I would've planned an extravagant evening with you in Annapolis in the exact spot where we first met, but the thing is... I don't want to recreate the memory of when we first became friends. I want to start something new with you. Something new right here in Solomons Island."

She dropped her purse and drew her hands up to her mouth.

"The second reason I brought you here is to ask you to be my wife. I know you have your fears... your so-called reasons why what we have is good enough. But, I'm sorry, I don't agree with you. Why settle for good enough when it can be magnificent? Don't you want magnificent? I'll never be able to replace your late husband, and I would never want to. But, I promise to love you and take care of you for the rest of our lives, Mae... even when you're acting like an old stubborn nag." He teased.

She sniffled a bit and gathered her composure. "Jonathan-"

"Hold on, I'm not finished yet. I'm sure you're wondering why I abruptly ended our week of silence. But, after taking the time to consider things, the truth is, I can't just let you go, Mae. You and me... we belong together. And, this whole deal with us doing better in our own living quarters and being used to our routines... that's not reason enough to be apart. Not in my book."

He opened the box and pulled out a gorgeous band made with diamonds and onyx, Mae's favorite stones. It wasn't your traditional engagement ring. But Mae wasn't your traditional kind of woman.

"Come closer." He humbly pleaded.

She took a few steps toward him, trying to hold back her emotions.

"Mae, will you marry me?"

She held her head down in shame.

"I don't know what to say." The words barely escaped her lips.

"Say yes."

She looked out over the water and then returned her attention to Jonathan.

"I... Jonathan, I'm so sorry. I had no idea you were planning this. The last thing I want to do is hurt you, but I really think we should go." She fumbled a few steps away, nervously picked up her purse, and walked as fast as she could, leaving Jonathan by the water.

~

"You left him on his knee?" Clara repeated.

"Yes, I panicked. I literally felt like I could have a nervous breakdown. I didn't want to just leave him like that, but it's like I couldn't bring myself to follow through and say yes. This is awful, isn't it?" Mae asked.

She continued to sob as they sat in the supply room, trying to make sense of everything that just happened. Clara always viewed Mae as the mature matriarch of the staff. She was wise, always stubborn, but level-headed, and always in control. That's why it shocked Clara to see her falling apart in the supply room of Lighthouse Tours. Thankfully, Jonathan dropped her off and had gone home for the day, and the rest of the guys were out back.

"Okay, breathe. Let's rewind this thing back to the beginning. Tell me everything that happened."

Mae tried to speak, though she was hyperventilating.

"Deep breath, Mae," she said to herself.

"I'll tell you what. You don't sound like a woman who really wanted to say no. I could almost understand this better if you were feeling a little sad. But,

I've never seen you like this before, Ms. Mae," Clara said.

"I know. Jonathan is my best friend, and it hurts me to think that I may have broken his heart."

"Then, why did you say no?"

"I didn't say no. I just didn't say anything. I ran away like a timid little child. I ought to be ashamed of myself. He was just trying to pour out his heart the best way he knew how," she said, holding a tissue over her face.

"So, you're afraid? Okay, that's totally normal." Clara suggested.

"It is?"

"Yes, this is your future we're talking about here. Haven't you ever heard of a runaway bride? In this case, you were more like the runaway... girlfriend? Maybe?" Clara teased.

Mae released a little laughter, but not enough to lift the burden of what just happened.

"I am such a fool. I know he's a good man, but he's right. I've allowed my fears to get in the way." Mae confessed.

"What are those fears? Let's identify them... get them out in the open so you can deal with them, already," Clara said.

"Oh, Clara. I feel terrible dragging you into this. You have your own life to deal with."

"You're not dragging me into anything. I chose to be back here, sitting on stools in a dusty old supply room with you. You didn't force me into anything. Now, stop thinking like that. From the moment I accepted this job at Lighthouse Tours, I felt like I was blessed with a new work family. I needed that more than anything, especially after losing Joan. Now, humor me... tell me what's troubling you," she said.

"I think it's the whole idea of getting married again and potentially losing my soulmate again. I can't bear that kind of pain twice. My husband left too soon. One morning he was right there, lying by my side, as he normally would be. We got up, ate our breakfast, and headed out to work... all was well. Later that afternoon, I received a call telling me he collapsed on the job and was being rushed to the emergency room." Mae looked upward while dabbing her eyes.

"I didn't make it in time to see him, Clara. He was already gone by the time I arrived. I can't go through that again. I can't do it."

She grabbed some more tissues.

"Subjecting myself to losing a mate again is more than I can bear. I'm sorry."

"Ms. Mae, you shouldn't apologize for the way you feel. Trust me. I understand what it's like to lose someone you love deeply," Clara said.

"But, your husband is still alive. He's crazy... but he's alive." Mae argued.

Clara couldn't disagree.

"True. I may not have lost a mate, but I lost both

my parents in a car accident. If that doesn't qualify, I don't know what does," she said.

"I'm so sorry. I didn't mean to-"

"That's all right. I know you meant nothing by it. The point I'm trying to make here is it's completely okay to feel afraid. As long as you don't allow your fear to stop you from living your life. I hate to put it this way, but we're all going to die someday. Who's to say you wouldn't go before Jonathan? We can't go around living our lives in fear. It's not healthy. If I lived my life like that, I'd still be stuck in New York with a crazy loon for a husband, missing my parents, and resentful that my sister and I don't have a better relationship. That's a whole other story that I'll save for another day." She smiled.

Mae let out a long sigh.

"I know everything you're saying is right. I guess I've just gotten used to playing it safe. I like my routines. I guess that makes me a bit of an old soul, but I don't care. My life is fine the way it is, and I don't know if I want to rock the boat."

Clara placed her hands on top of Mae's and leaned in to comfort her.

"I have one question for you to consider. Can you picture yourself living a life without him? A life by yourself with your comfortable routines... and no Jonathan?"

Mae looked toward the small window in the back of the room. "No," she said in a soft voice.

"Well, then, get your man."

"How can I face him after today? He's probably mortified," Mae said.

"The only way you'll know is if you talk to him. Trust me, his ego may be bruised, but there's no way he stopped loving you that quickly. Now, get up, go splash your face with water, and go get your man. Tell him you're sorry... blame it on temporary insanity if you have to."

Mae chuckled hard enough to make her belly jiggle.

"I don't know if he'll fall for that one," she said.

"Well, then, tell him fear caused you to panic. It's not like you'd be lying. Be transparent with him. Jonathan will come around," Clara said.

Mae drew in a big breath.

"I will, Clara. Thank you for this little talk. I'm usually the one who has it together but today I completely fell apart." Mae admitted.

"I don't know anybody who has it all together, Ms. Mae. Whenever you need someone to talk to, just know you have a shoulder to lean on, okay?"

"Clara, the same offer is extended to you. I feel completely selfish pouring out my heart and crying like a baby, when you're going through so much," Mae said.

Mae stood and opened up her arms to give Clara a hug.

"Don't you worry about me. I'm sure they'll be

plenty of opportunities for us to have future supply room meetings to discuss my issues. We'll catch up later. But, for now, get going. Tomorrow, I want to hear all about it."

Mae blew a kiss Clara's way and left her in the supply room.

~

That afternoon Clara was immersed in directing a large party of guests who would join Tommy for the two-hour lighthouse tour. She was also knee deep in a ton of receipts generated from Brody's shopping sprees to assist Mike in opening the new store. She missed Mike's presence in the office but was distracted by an incoming call from her lawyer.

"Kolton, I wasn't expecting to hear from you so soon. What's the good word?" Clara asked.

"Hi, Clara. I'm heading into court, so I won't keep you. I just thought you'd be excited to know we're filing the papers as early as next week. My assistant has been digging around and doing some research. As far as we can tell, Keith doesn't have a leg to stand on. It looks like he's suffering financially. The bank put a lien on his property, and the debt collector has been on his trail for months and months of back payments on the car, credit cards, you name it. The guy was trying to cash out when he paid you a visit here in Maryland. I think we have a solid case to proceed forward with the divorce. As for the inheritance, as I mentioned, that's not marital property, so you should be good to go. The only other thing I would be diligent about is seeing that all your account numbers, passwords, and anything else he could've possibly had access to from the past is secure. It may be a tedious task but call each institution and change every password if you have to... just to be certain."

"Yes, of course. Why didn't I think of that prior to now?" Clara said.

"It's okay. The likelihood that he can do anything with your accounts is minimal, but since we don't know how he found out about your funds, there's no harm in being safe."

"I completely agree," she said.

"Are you free to come by the office and fill out some paperwork on Monday, around five?"

"Five o'clock is perfect," Clara responded.

"Great, I'll have my assistant email the forms to you so you can start reviewing them over the weekend. I will share any remaining documents with you on Monday. Our address and suite number will be on the letterhead," he said.

"Great. Thanks again."

CHAPTER 11

"*P*lease remind me... why did I decide to open another store again?" Mike asked.

"You opened the store because you're a man with vision. You wanted to expand your horizons and-" Clara tried to build Mike up, but exhaustion was starting to settle in and he wasn't having it.

"Okay, I know why. The better question is, why didn't I see that I'm getting older now, I'm exhausted, and I may have bitten off more than I can chew?" he said, sounding defeated.

"Let's be reasonable here. The new business hasn't even been open for a week yet. Exhaustion comes with the territory. This is totally normal," she said, trying to reassure him.

"Yes, but we didn't expect so many people on opening day. I'm literally running on fumes."

Clara positioned her cell phone between her shoulder and ear, walking from door to door, ensuring the house was secure for the evening. She wanted to ask Mike when he'd be free to come and visit. She wanted to experience kissing him on the beach again, but instead of saying it, she just listened.

"Don't get me wrong. I'm so thankful for the tremendous response from the community. I wish you could've been there. We even had folks signing up for some of the fall tours. It was amazing," he said.

"See, that's what I'm talking about. That's the spirit."

"Yeah, how was everything at the Solomons office today? Did the schedule run smoothly as planned?" he asked.

"We didn't have any problems. Tommy pretty much ran the show with the tours today, and I think Jonathan is on tomorrow morning, and Ms. Mae in the afternoon. The two of them are at odds this week, but I'm sure Jonathan will share his version with you whenever he gets around to it. By the way, I locked up everything like you asked. Oh, and I started going through Brody's receipts. Mike, there has to be a better way for us to keep track of purchases. I thought you were planning to upgrade that whole system months ago?" She complained.

"Clara..."

"Yes?"

"I know you've probably had a long day, but I

called because I miss you. I feel like you and I still have some unfinished business to take care of," he said.

"Oh, really. What kind of unfinished business are you referring to?" She flirted, fully enjoying where he was going with the conversation.

"The kind of unfinished business between two people who've been waiting to be together."

"Be together, how?" she asked.

"In a relationship... and in other ways, too."

"What do you propose we do about this dilemma we're facing?" Clara spoke softly and somewhat flirtatiously.

"I propose we never let another evening go by without me coming over and kissing you goodnight. I don't want the days to pass without seeing your beautiful smile. Seeing you gives me something to look forward to," he said.

She bit her bottom lip and fantasized about what it would be like.

"Are you still there?" he asked.

"I'm here. So, you literally want to come over every single night? Come on, Mike. Be realistic. You're already exhausted and you're not even a week into the new schedule," she said.

"Don't you worry about me. Just let me come over and see you while the night is still young. I promise I won't keep you up long." He begged.

"All right. How long will it take for you to get here?"

"I can be there in thirty to forty minutes, tops," he said. She could hear the engine of the jeep turning over in the background, motivating her to head toward the shower.

"I'll see you then."

Clara lathered her strawberry hair in shampoo while allowing the hot water to wash away the stress of the day. Relaxing in the shower was one of her nightly rituals after coming in from the beach. At least she tried to relax, but this evening her mind was busy with thoughts like, *What should I wear? Oh, don't be ridiculous, Clara. He doesn't care about what you're wearing. Just play it cool and put on something casual.*

She continued to scrub. *Oh, man. What if things elevate to the next level between us? I haven't been with a man in so long I don't even know...* Before completing her thought, she shook it off and sped things along. The last thing she wanted to do was convince herself that tonight wasn't a good idea.

Outside the shower, Holly waited patiently with a tennis ball in her mouth.

"Look at you, sweet girl. Always ready to play, aren't you?" Clara said.

She stood in front of the closet with her head wrapped in a towel, flipping through various pieces of clothing before deciding on jean shorts and summer t-shirt.

"What do you think, Holly? How about I brush my hair and go with the wet look, dab some light concealer under these eyes, a little foundation, some blush, a little lipstick, and call it a day? We like to keep it as low maintenance as possible, don't we girl?"

Clara continued talking and playing with Holly while getting ready. She hoped that effortless beauty would win Mike over, especially since their gathering was impromptu and on a work night.

She retreated to the kitchen, realizing she hadn't eaten and if she knew right, Mike would probably be hungry as well.

"I guess I could throw a couple of steaks on the grill." She reconsidered, still feeling uneasy about being outside at night by herself. She knew it was silly, but the effects of Keith's unannounced visits still lingered in the back of her mind. She hoped she could shake the thoughts and get back to normal soon.

Broiled steaks will have to do. Maybe I can throw in baked potatoes and asparagus, she thought.

Pellets of rain began beating down on the roof, serving as further reassurance that outdoor dining would have to wait for another time. With the oven set to her desired temperature, the meat seasoned, and sides that required light prep, Clara was ready for a glass of wine and ready to welcome her late-night guest.

Holly sounded her natural alarm when the door-bell rang. Running around in circles and announcing a stranger's arrival to the neighborhood was something she did very well.

Clara unlocked the door and swung it open, ready to fuss at Mike for driving so fast in the rain. On the other side of the door he stood, drenched, with his abs showing through his white shirt. He looked amazing. So good, she had to remember to snap out of her staring frenzy and invite him in.

"How did you get here so fast?" she asked while helping Holly to settle down.

He came inside, looking down at his clothing in disgust.

"I guess the idea of seeing you motivated me. I would've rung the doorbell sooner if I didn't notice that my front tire looks flat. Hence, the reason I'm soaking wet," he said.

"Man, your entire outfit is soaking wet," she said.

"I don't have men's clothing for you to wear, but I can offer you a dryer if you want to strip down and dry your clothes." Clara laughed, finding the idea of him having to walk around in the buff rather amusing.

"I'm glad you're having so much fun with this.

Do you know what it feels like to walk around in wet pants and a wet shirt?" he asked.

"I've been there a time or two. It's definitely not fun." She teased.

"Follow me. You can shower in the guest's room upstairs to your right. There's an oversized guest's robe folded in the linen closet that you can wear until your clothes dry. You can leave the squeaky shoes at the front door."

"Funny. I don't think I've ever taken you as a guest's robe kind of woman," he said.

"Ha, I'm really not. Joan used to always keep a new set of robes and slippers on hand whenever she would entertain. She stopped having many people over during the last few years, but she always made sure the house was fully stocked." She explained.

She led him upstairs and pointed him in the right direction.

"I threw some steaks in the oven if you're hungry. Feel free to use the shower. I'll be downstairs once you're finished."

He took a step closer, kissed her hand, and disappeared into the guest room.

They laughed over dinner at stories surrounding his first day mishaps at the new store. They sipped wine and Clara admired the sight of Mike sitting across the table in a white terrycloth robe.

"Not exactly the look I was going for this evening, but I am grateful for the use of your dryer and a hot shower," he said.

"I think you look cute, to be honest. But, what are you going to do about your tire?"

"The rain will let up soon. When it does, I'll run out and switch to the spare. Dinner is great, by the way. I didn't expect you to do all this, but I sure could get used to it," he said.

"I'll bet. Next time you're cooking for me."

"I don't know about the cooking part, but I'll order the finest meal in town and deliver it to you nice and hot." He offered.

"It's a deal."

He stared into Clara's eyes. "Thank you," he said.

"You already thanked me for the meal. It was no big deal. I was happy to throw something together."

"No. For this moment. Allowing me to come here and be with you. It's kind of crazy, but today was a really big day for me, and somehow all I could manage to think about was you. You're doing something to me, Clara. I can tell you right now, if you're really not that interested in me, you should say something now, before I fall in too deep." Mike said it jokingly, but she knew he was serious.

She put her glass down.

"How do you know it's not just a passing desire?

Or some brief infatuation that will dissipate the moment we get too close?" she asked.

Without hesitation Mike responded, "Because the last time a woman made me feel this way was when I met my fiancé. I haven't met anybody like her until now. Not one."

"Tell me about her. What was she like? What made you fall in love with her?" Clara asked while clearing the plates off the table.

"You sure?" he asked.

"Yeah, I want to know what you saw in her."

"All right." He cleared the rest of the items on the table and followed her to the kitchen sink.

"Just like yourself, she was drop dead gorgeous, but never acted like she knew it. She was humble and had a big heart of gold. Again, just like you. She came from wealth, but you'd never know it. She couldn't care less about what was in her trust fund and the millions her family was worth. The proof was in her level of service to our country. I never could understand why someone who had it all would sign up to serve in the coast guard. But, she did," Mike said.

"Wow. I must look like I had a silver spoon handed to me from your point of view. I'm not hardly doing anything as honorable as serving in the military."

"Clara, if that's the way you view yourself, then your vision is cloudy. Look in the mirror. You received an inheritance and still continue to work a nine-to-five job that you don't technically need. You drive an old beat up Honda Accord-"

"Hey, don't talk about Bessy like that. She's good to me, thank you very much." She laughed.

He raised his hands in surrender.

"I apologize. I didn't mean to offend you or Bessy, but you know what I mean. Unless somebody knows you or has visited your home, they'd never know about your wealth. They'd only see your humble and loving personality. That's attractive to me. It's one of the reasons I fell for my fiancé. You can only imagine how much it broke my heart to lose her when she died."

"I'm really sorry, Mike." Clara loved how candid he was, and she adored his willingness to become so vulnerable.

She stepped aside, watching him as he took over at the sink. Standing barefoot and in a robe, he washed the dishes and towel dried them. He only allowed her to assist when he needed help to put everything away.

She paused, admiring how comfortable he was in his own skin and in her home. There was no getting around it. She wasn't ready to say it out loud, but she enjoyed having him there.

"Tell me more. What was her family like, and did you stay in touch after?" she asked.

"Uh, let's see. Her folks warmed up to me, eventually. But it took a while. I wasn't exactly what they hand in mind for their daughter at first glance. I think they were more into the white-collar, Wall Street type."

"They didn't find it admirable that you served our country?" she asked.

"Sure, they did. As long as it didn't involve me getting too serious about their daughter. I think secretly they had high hopes that she'd give up on military life and come back home, maybe even get involved in the family business," he responded.

"Ah, I see. If only they could see you now. You're a successful business owner."

"Hmm, I don't think it would've mattered. We didn't stay in touch long after the funeral. I returned some of her belongings to them and kept a few pieces of memorabilia, but after that, I haven't heard from them. Of course, that was so long ago now, I wouldn't expect to," he said.

"It's such a shame no one thought to check and see how you were doing."

"Yep, well, thankfully that's where therapy came in handy. What about your folks? What were they like?" Mike asked.

Clara walked over to the glass doors that faced the dock in the rear of the house.

"Hardworking. Dad worked his way up the chain in the postal system. Mom was a hairdresser. They got up before the break of day and always saw that my sister and I had school supplies, clothing, shoes with good soles, and a hot meal at the start and end of each day. They were traditional. They taught us to mind our manners, go to church on Sunday, and look out for our neighbors. Occasionally, if we were good, they allowed us to treat ourselves to something from the neighborhood ice cream truck." She laughed.

"Man, those were the good old days. I miss them. I often think of how they'd still be here today if they hadn't encountered a drunk driver."

"That's terrible. Yet, it's probably part of the reason you're so strong, so resilient, and a fighter when you need to be. I watched the way you faced your ex head on. Few would be brave enough to do the same," he replied.

Clara felt Mike's hands cup her shoulders, sending chills over her body. She didn't turn around but could hear him breathing in the scent of her hair as he kissed her by the ear.

"Do you remember that moment we had together on the beach the other night?" she asked.

"How could I forget?"

"I was thinking about it before you got here, hoping we could pick up where we left off. If it's all right with you, of course." The wine helped Clara to relax and speak freely. It had been ten years since she allowed herself to be free to love. She wanted Mike and was finally ready to stop putting her love life on hold.

He chuckled. "Normally, I'd jump at the opportunity in a heartbeat. But, have you seen what I'm wearing? If I step any closer to you, I'm afraid of what might happen."

She turned to him. "I'm not afraid."

The rain quieted down, leaving subtle flashes of lightning lingering in the distance. Each flash highlighted his broad shoulders towering over her as they embraced.

CHAPTER 12

*M*ae pulled her famous crab dip from the refrigerator, and offered it with some chips and a refreshing beverage to Jonathan, who was sitting at her center island. It was normally one of his favorite snacks to indulge in after work. Today he didn't seem to have much of an appetite. She placed a few napkins on the table and paced around the kitchen, making small talk while seeing that everything was tidy.

"Mae, I thought you asked me to stop by because you had something you wanted to talk about," he said.

"I do," she said nervously, pulling the broom out of the pantry and sweeping around the floor.

"I wanted to talk with you about the other day."

With very little to sweep, Mae finished up a small

area and returned the broom to the closet. She dusted off her clothes and took a deep breath. Jonathan had a no nonsense expression on his face and barely made eye-contact.

"You don't have to explain. I misjudged the situation. Perhaps put too much thought into it and overstepped my boundaries. You don't have to worry. It won't happen again."

She stopped breathing for a moment.

"I asked you to come over because I need to take ownership of what I've done. I owe you an apology, Jonathan," she said.

"You don't owe me anything. You don't want to get married, I get it. I'm just sorry I created such an awkward situation between us. I'm hoping it's not too late to recover from it... I mean, we do still have to work together and all. I was hoping we could bring closure to this whole thing and move on," he responded.

Mae drew back, feeling surprised by his response. He was normally the type to put up a fight and go after what he wanted. But not this time. He was stone-cold and distant.

What has gotten into him? she thought.

"So, am I to assume that you no longer have feelings for me? I can't just stand here and pretend you didn't propose to me, Jonathan."

"I'm not asking you to pretend. But, I am asking

you, for the sake of our work relationship, that we make amends and move on," he said.

"How dare you?" Mae asked.

"Me? How dare I what?"

"How dare you take on such a nonchalant attitude about this like it's no big deal, Jonathan? You just proposed. Do you really want me to believe that you suddenly don't care anymore? We could never just make amends and move on like nothing ever happened," she said.

"Mae, I mean this in the most respectful way, but have you lost your mind? I'm the underdog here, not you. I invested in a ring, surprised you at work, took you to the beach, and poured my heart out to you... and now you're fussing at me about being nonchalant? Give me a break. How do you expect me to act? I'm still trying to pick my face off the ground from the humiliation of watching you run away from me. I keep replaying that image over and over in my mind. Do you think it's easy for me to face you after experiencing something like that? I barely worked up the nerve to come over here today."

"I know, and I'm sorry for being the one to cause you so much pain. I could've responded differently. I could've been more upfront about what was bothering me," she said.

"Do you think?" he said, snapping open the can of Coke she left on the counter for him.

"So, now that you have me here. Tell me, what did I do to cause you to run off like that?"

"It wasn't you, Jonathan. I let my fear get in the way," she said.

"You? Fear? Mae, you can do better than that. You're built like a tough machine ready to combat any and everything head on. I can't imagine what you would be afraid of."

"Well, that's just it. Just because I'm strong-willed doesn't mean I always have it together. Did you ever consider how hard it might be for someone like myself to marry again, for fear of losing another soulmate?" she asked with a timid look in her eyes.

Jonathan's shoulders relaxed as if the grief of what she said took over his whole being.

"No. I didn't consider it," he responded.

"I know I shouldn't allow fear to run my life. But, I panicked and unfortunately, I ran. It's no excuse for my actions, but you deserve to know the truth. It was never about you, Jonathan," she said.

"Well, now I know. But, I can't say I feel any better. It sounds like the one woman I truly love will never be available to love me in return and that hurts like hell, Mae."

Jonathan stood up and pushed his stool in. While still holding on to the wooden frame, he closed his eyes and spoke.

"I feel bad for everything you've been through. I really do. But, you're going to miss out on some beautiful life experiences based on the fear of what may or may not happen. That's no way to live."

He looked at her one last time with sadness in his eyes and then began heading toward the front door. Mae's lip trembled. She had a feeling once he walked out that door, he wouldn't return.

"Jonathan, wait." She desperately called out.

At Kolton's law firm, Clara held his Montblanc pen to sign the last papers to get the divorce proceedings underway. As she formed each letter in cursive, it felt like she was signing a rite of passage or declaration to regain her freedom. Ten years of holding on to a marriage that wasn't worth mentioning, and now it was finally dissipating with a few strokes of a pen.

"Where else do I need to sign?" she asked.

"You're all set. From the look on your face, I take it you're feeling pretty good about what we went over this afternoon?"

"I couldn't be more pleased. It still amazes me I waited this long. But, I'm ready now. More ready than I've ever been." She withdrew her sunglasses from her purse and positioned them to hold her hair back.

"Clara, may I offer you a little advice, off the record?" Kolton asked.

"Sure."

"You're an attractive woman, single, wealthy, and to be honest, Keith will not be the last person in your life who shows up looking to get their piece of the pie. Next time, it could be a stranger, a family member, or even another guy. Do yourself a favor and protect your assets. I know a woman who's a great financial advisor and could probably give you some tips and help you out. It's my guess that you're not used to having this kind of money, and I'd hate to see anybody else show up and try to take advantage of you," he said.

She noticed Kolton's pristine appearance, sleek haircut, cuff links, and office filled with more mahogany wood than the law should allow. She felt somewhat exposed, knowing the only reason she could afford to be there was because of the money she inherited. Otherwise, she'd be scrambling to scrape two pennies together to pay for a lawyer the same way Keith was.

"Thank you, Kolton. I'll keep that in mind." She backed away from the table and put her sunglasses on.

"Are we all set?" she asked.

"Yes, you are free to go. If all goes well, and there's no appeal, the judge can sign off on this in thirty days."

"And if he appeals?" she asked.

"Let's think positive and cross that hurdle if it

comes down to it. If you're feeling pretty confident that Keith's all talk, then let's go with that for now."

Clara's stomach knotted up at the thought of the unknown. She didn't think Keith had the funds to hire someone to make her life miserable, but she couldn't be certain of anything.

"Clara, let me worry about the details. I will call you if anything changes," he said.

"Right. Thanks, Kolton."

"No problem." He walked her to the lobby and held the front door.

"Remember, try not to worry."

She wasn't certain she'd adhere to his advice, but for now she'd try to do her best.

Back in the car, she played a voice message from Mike. *"Hey, Clara, just wanted to remind you that dinner is on me tonight. I'm bringing crab cakes from Mel's in North Beach, as requested. Can't wait to see you. Oh, don't let me forget to tell you about an idea that I have for the assistant manager position. See you soon."*

She turned over the ignition and checked her rearview.

This feels right.

She pulled out of the space, heading home to be with her man.

~

~

~

Back at Mae's, Jonathan had one hand on the door-knob, ready to leave. He'd suffered enough, and she could fully understand it if he didn't want to put up with her anymore. Who could blame him? But it didn't stop her from making one last plea for him to listen.

"Jonathan, I know I have my hang-ups, but I need you to believe that I love you and I really want you in my life."

"You could've fooled me. That's not the impression I received when I proposed," he said.

"I can't imagine my life without you in it. Please, believe me. I mean it from the bottom of my heart."

He continued to stand with his hand on the door-knob and his head hanging low. After a moment, he let his hand drop but wouldn't turn around.

"You want us to be together under your conditions, Mae. Think about the last few serious conversations we've had. You're quick to remind me of how I can come spend the night with you, but I can't live with you. Then, you'll tell me you're accustomed to living a certain way, and it's better we don't upset what we're used to. These are your words, not mine. That doesn't sound like a woman who will ever entertain being married. Now that I think of it, I was taking a major leap when I proposed. I thought the romantic gesture would've won you over, but I should've known the odds were stacked against me. Now, this evening, you tell me you're afraid to lose a soulmate again. I feel for you. But, if I can't do anything that will provide you with some sense of comfort and cause you to welcome me with open arms, then why bother? You don't need me. You sound more and more like a woman who wants to be alone."

She placed her hand on the back of his shoulder.

"That's simply not true. I want you. Jonathan, I need you in my life. You mean the world to me. If I have to spend every day proving that to you, I will." She confessed.

He wiped his face and opened the door. "Don't bother. I already tried proving it to you first, and it didn't work. I can't see how anything could possibly change now."

She watched Jonathan walk out the door and make his way toward his pickup. It was a scene she had witnessed before and it made her heart sink. She felt a lump rising in her throat. She had really done it this time and felt clueless about what she could do to get him to come back.

She stood there, frozen, watching his truck pull away, feeling consumed with shame and defeat.

After several minutes, she closed the door. Mae could hear the phone ringing in the background but felt depleted and didn't answer. Her daughter's voice bellowed through the answering machine, leaving a message about coming to Solomons to visit. Normally, Mae would be thrilled, but tonight she needed to pull herself together and recover from a broken heart.

CHAPTER 13

Food covered every ounce of Clara's kitchen counter, ranging from barbecue to delightful summer salads. She invited Mackenzie, and her friend, Bill, to cook out with her and Mike on Saturday evening. It was like having a double date at home and a chance for the guys to bond while the ladies played catch up with one another.

"Mack, I have to say, the more I spend time around Bill, the more I really like him for you. He seems like such a good guy," she said while flipping the grilled chicken.

Mack sighed. "That means a lot to me, Clara. Thank you. He is a nice guy, isn't he? It's been great having him around."

"Has he met Stephanie yet?" Clara asked.

"No. I want him to meet her, but I'm struggling with how to go about it. I've always protected Steph from meeting anyone that I date for obvious reasons. I don't want her to be confused or even upset if the relationship doesn't work out."

"That makes sense, but if things are progressing with you two, you can't keep Bill a secret forever. Don't you think he's going to ask questions?" Clara carefully mixed and applied another layer of her mother's famous barbecue recipe to the chicken while they continued to talk.

"He's already started asking questions. Bill is family oriented. He has a daughter of his own who's in college, but he works hard to make sure her tuition is paid and she has everything she needs. He's such a wonderful dad, so it's only natural that he would want to get to know my sweet girl. Thankfully, he doesn't push me on the subject. But, eventually, if things keep going the way they have been, I'll need to arrange a time for them to meet."

"Do tell. How have things been going?" Clara asked.

"Words cannot describe how happy I am. I keep wondering if it's all a dream that will eventually end with some sort of rude awakening."

"Oh my goodness, will you stop, Mack? Be positive and just enjoy the ride. You deserve true happiness for a change. Not to say you weren't happy before Bill came along, but you are literally glowing."

Mackenzie unraveled the saran wrap covering her antipasto salad and helped arrange the plates and utensils on the table.

"I'm not the only one who's glowing. When you called to invite us over, I was so glad to hear that Mike would join us. You two seem extra cozy with one another. Did I miss something?" Mack suggested.

"Nothing out of the ordinary." Clara smirked.

"You better step to the side so you don't get struck by lightning for telling such a lie. Something is different between you two. Now spill it before I bring the subject up during dinner and embarrass you right in front of Mike."

"You wouldn't dare," Clara said.

"Try me. Now hurry and tell me before they come out here."

"We've been seeing each other more regularly as of late." Clara peered over her shoulder to make sure the coast was clear.

"He's been so romantic. He stops by every night after he closes up the shop just to see me before the night concludes. Last night, he brought me dinner, and we talked and talked. It was amazing," Clara said, beaming from ear to ear.

"He comes by every night? Wow. To think you didn't believe me in the beginning when I said you two would be a good fit for each other. I know how to call a spade when I see one."

Clara flipped the meat over for the last time and

sat down to enjoy some cocktails. She loved having company and entertaining. Watching the guys bond over beers inside the kitchen filled her up on the inside. If there was a heaven, which she believed there was, she hoped Joan was looking down, proud of how things were turning out at the beach house.

"Have you two been turning up the heat at night?" Mackenzie asked.

"Haven't you heard the saying, a lady never kisses and tells?"

"Oh, please. Must you be so proper?" Mack scolded her.

"Well, if you must know. We haven't done anything... yet," she responded.

"Oh, but I hear the hesitation in your voice, honey. You want to do something!"

"I definitely check the temperature in the house whenever he comes over. It always feels like something is wrong with the air conditioner when in reality it's just Mike making me feel so..."

"Hot and bothered!" Mack blurted out and laughed so hard she had to squeeze her legs together to maintain control.

"Mack, hush. The guys are looking this way. See. That's why I can't tell you anything." She sniggled.

"Well, it's true. He's probably setting off all the bells, whistles, and sensors in your body that haven't been operating for a mighty long time. It's been ten long years for goodness' sake," Mack said.

"Gee, thanks for the reminder. Let's talk about something else. The guys are coming this way."

The men joined them outdoors, each holding their beers, making themselves comfortable at the table. Bill referenced the outdoor fireplace while placing his arm around Mackenzie. He thought it would make a great spot for outdoor gatherings in the fall.

"Clara, you sure have a lovely home. I could easily envision myself roasting marshmallows over the fireplace and spending lots of quality time out here on your private beach."

"Thanks, Bill. You and Mack are welcome to come hang out here any time. If you like the water, then I'm happy to let you two borrow the boat for the day and take it for a spin."

"That would be nice," Mackenzie replied.

"Sounds like a great idea for our next date night. Or we can make it a double date. I bet Mike could show us the ropes, couldn't you, Mike?" Bill asked.

"Sorry, no can do, buddy. My date gets seasick," he said, smiling at Clara.

"Wait, let me get this straight. Clara, you own a boat, but you get seasick?" he asked.

"Pretty much. Trust me, if I hadn't inherited the boat, we wouldn't be having this conversation. I just can't bring myself to sell it. Joan always felt the same way about it. She never wanted to throw away the precious memories. To be honest, neither do I. I've established my own memories over time. For example, look over there, toward the boat slip. That entire area leading out to the dock is where I spent all of my down time as her housekeeper. I'd mainly daydream, sketch in my notepad, or try to think and plan out my future. It's such a peaceful place to get lost in your thoughts and relax. At one point, I even started making plans for opening my own business someday," she said.

"I never knew you desired to start your own business," Mike said.

Clara smiled and then brushed off the idea.

"Yeah, it wasn't a big deal. To this day, if you asked me exactly what type of business, I still couldn't tell you. I listed several from starting my own housekeeping company, to buying out the café. I was just dreaming, that's all."

"If you owned the café, then at least we would all interact with the owner more. I swear the new owner stops by, maybe once every couple of months, if that," Mack responded.

"Really?"

"Yeah, it's the strangest thing I've ever seen. His accountant runs that place more than he does. I guess if nothing else, he cares about his money. I just think it would be nice if he were more present," Mack said.

Bill weighed in, complementing Mack on the wonderful job she was doing running the place.

Meanwhile, Clara noticed Mike admiring her, giving her a friendly, yet flirtatious wink, causing her to wish they were alone.

"Well, Clara, I still think if you have an inkling of a desire to own your own business someday, you should explore the idea every chance you get. In the meantime, I was kind of hoping you'd consider the idea I brought up before I left last night. I think it would be great practice, should you ever decide to go down the ownership route," Mike said.

"Ooh, what kind of opportunity, if I'm not being too nosey," Mack asked.

"Mike asked me to consider expanding my office assistant work to include assistant manager responsibilities. You know, to help keep things afloat when he's at the new location," she responded.

"No, if we're going to tell it, tell it right. I said to Clara that I've noticed how she has a knack for overseeing the schedule, helping me with the books, putting out fires, and seeing that things run smoothly when I'm not around. That gave me the idea to use Clara for the role." Mike proudly shared.

Clara served everyone's plate and passed out corn holders for the corn on the cob. She pulled another round of beer out of the cooler for the guys and refilled, making sure everything was just so, before sitting down to tell her side of the story.

"I tried to tell Mike that I already happily do

those things and didn't think it was necessary to make a big fuss over it. I'd hate for the staff to think that I'm receiving some sort of preferential treatment," she said.

"But, Clara, you would do the things they don't have time for. Their focus is to run the boat tours. I'm with Mike. If you have the skills, why not put them to good use?" Mack said.

"Thank you, Mack! That's exactly what I was thinking. Plus, I didn't plan on hitting her over the head with taking on the assistant manager role at once. I figured we could groom and prep her over the next six months to a year. That way, she could take her time learning the various tasks, and it would give us the time to ensure it's a good fit." Mike agreed.

"Sounds like a win, win situation if you ask me." Mack smiled.

"Bill, do you see what I have to go through when I spend too much time with these two? They both have a way of talking you into just about anything. Keep your eye on this one over here," she said, referring to Mack.

"Hey, I always have your back and you know it," Mack said.

"Yes, you do. And, Mike, I know you do, too. You've always given me a chance. Matter of fact, from the first day we met, life has been filled with nothing but opportunities and second chances with you. Thank you for that," she said.

"You've thanked me a thousand times. When your discernment tells you that you've found a good thing, you hold on to it. You never let a good thing go."

She took another bite of her food, feeling pretty certain he was referring to more than just her skills as an employee. With the sun setting in the backdrop and butterflies settling in the pit of her stomach, Clara knew she was falling in love.

On Monday morning Mae dragged her feet in around eleven, seemingly downtrodden, and not much in the mood for small talk. Her first tour wasn't scheduled until noon, but normally she had more to say, which gave Clara a clue that things didn't exactly go according to plan with Jonathan.

Clara subtly tiptoed around the subject looking for the right opportunity to bring it up.

"How was your weekend, Ms. Mae?" she asked.

"Uneventful. Yours?"

"It was lovely. I had a few friends over for dinner. We grilled out back and watched the sun go down. Grilling is actually becoming one of my favorite ways to cook these days."

"That's nice," Mae said in a monotone voice.

"So, did you do any gardening? I know how much you love getting out there and running your fingers through the soil. I wish I had a green thumb like you."

"No, wasn't feeling up to it." She glanced at her mailbox only to discover it was empty.

"Are you all right?" Clara asked.

"I'm fine. Just a little tired, that's all. I'll be in the back if anybody is looking for me." She disappeared, not even bothering to make her usual cup of coffee to start her day.

Clara pulled her rolling chair back over to her desk and flipped through a few emails. Most of them she could delete, but she tackled all inquiries from customers asking about upcoming summer tours. It would be another week before Mike returned to the office, but it still didn't stop her from thinking about him, wishing that he was there.

"Is Jonathan coming in today?" Mae startled Clara from behind.

"No, he won't be back until the morning. He called in sick, but thankfully, Tommy was free to take over his tours."

"Oh, I see."

"Ms. Mae, it's obvious something is bothering you. Did you have a talk with him, and if so, how did it go?"

"Not too well, Clara. I asked him to come to my place to sit down and talk, but somehow I still screwed things up, big time. I tried my best to be honest with him and confess where I went wrong. I apologized, and I told him about my fears. But, it didn't make a difference. He wasn't accepting anything I had to say. He thinks all hope is lost, and if that's the way he really feels about it, then I guess I have to go along with it, even if I don't agree," she replied.

"I'm so sorry to hear that. Did you mention he came over to your place?"

"Yes, I prepared his favorite snack, and we sat in the kitchen and talked. I thought surely things would turn out well, but they didn't."

"That's interesting. Maybe he just needs a little time. How many men do you know who would come over in the first place if they weren't still invested in hearing what you have to say? No matter what he's telling you, it's clear he cares for you," Clara said.

"I guess. If that's the case, he's going to get all the time he needs. It was difficult opening up to him and admitting all my shortcomings, and it got me nowhere. I don't think I'll be doing that anymore." Mae leaned on the counter, sulking. It made sense why she came in to work, acting out of sorts.

"Well, I better go pull myself together. The last thing my clients need is a depressed tour guide. It's not a good look for business," she said.

"No, it's not. However, I do have an idea that may help turn things around in the right direction for you." Clara offered.

"What's that?"

"Maybe he needs to see a grand gesture from you. You know, something that shows him just how much you love him." Clara's face lit up at the idea that was coming to mind.

"Clara, I don't know."

"Ms. Mae, hear me out first, then you can decide whether it's a good idea. We both know how much Jonathan loves you. Everything he's ever done for you speaks to his love and then some. So, how about you return the favor? What if you create a reenactment of the proposal on the beach?" Clara asked.

"He wouldn't fall for that. I doubt he'd be willing to go anywhere or do anything with me. The man hasn't called me all weekend after walking out of my house the other day. Nice try, but you'll need to come up with something better than that."

Clara laughed to herself. *How did I get the assignment of coming up with something better?* she thought.

"Okay, then, we'll just have to arrange it so he doesn't know what he's walking into. You know, like a surprise," she said.

"What do you mean? You want me to propose to Jonathan, except make it a surprise?"

"That's the general idea. You can recreate the proposal down at the beach in my backyard. He'll never see it coming. I can make up some reason to have him over... maybe to help look at Joan's old boat and see if he can start it up and get it running for me.

Of course, he may never forgive me once he figures out it was all a facade, but if you desperately want him back, it may be worth taking a risk." Clara nodded.

"No, thank you. I'm not proposing to anybody. That's not how momma taught us growing up, and I'm not about to change the rules now. If he doesn't want me, then so be it. But, the proper way is for a man to propose to a woman." Mae complained.

"Ms. Mae, you've got to be kidding me, right? Hey, I'll be the first to admit that I love a traditional man. I'll take a traditional man who believes in chivalry any day of the week. But, that's not what this was about. Jonathan did everything he was supposed to, and you rejected him, remember? So, now it's your turn if you want to get your man back. You don't have to get down on your knees if don't want to. Although, it might be a nice touch. But, you have to pour every ounce of your heart out until he takes you back... and I know he will. That's what you want, isn't it?" she asked.

"Well, yes, but-"

"Nope. No buts. It's now or never," Clara said, sounding assertive.

Mae contemplated for a while.

"I had no intention of dragging you in the middle of this. Let me think it over while I'm on my tour and get back to you."

"Okay, but, I wouldn't think about it too long if I were you."

Mae nodded and exited to the back, leaving Clara to return to a large stack of paperwork.

CHAPTER 14

Clara closed her driver's side door and briefly checked her reflection in the window. She ruffled her hair a bit and smoothed out her clothing, while balancing a surprise order of Mexican food and a large drink for lunch. Mike wasn't expecting her, but she thought it would be the perfect surprise.

When she walked in, Savannah was sitting at the front desk, welcoming her with a huge grin.

"Clara, I didn't expect to see you here. How are you?" she asked.

"Savannah?"

"Yes, don't be silly. As many times as I stopped by to see Mike in Solomons Island, I know you remember who I am," she replied.

"I remember. I just didn't realize you were working here, that's all."

"Oh, Mike didn't tell you? That's odd. I don't know how he could forget to mention it. We spend so many hours here every day, plus I consider myself to be rather unforgettable." She smirked.

"Right. Look, if you could just point me toward his office, then I can get out of your hair. I'm sure you have plenty of work to do," Clara said.

"It's really not that busy right now. I can walk you to the back."

"That's unnecessary, Savannah. I wanted to surprise Mike. Again, if you'll just point me in the right direction, I'll be on my way."

Savannah pointed down the hallway to her right while inspecting the lunch in Clara's hand. Clara admired the old town fishing store feeling the place gave her. Ordinarily she'd explore, but Savannah's presence made her wish she hadn't come. She walked down the hallway, noticing the wooden anchor on the wall and the rustic decor. When she arrived at the door labeled with Mike's name, she knocked.

"Come in," he responded.

She poked her head in, making sure he wasn't occupied.

"Hey," she said.

"Clara, wow, come on in. I wasn't expecting you," he said.

"If you were expecting me, then it wouldn't be a surprise."

"A surprise?" he asked.

She held up a large sweet tea and an order of quesadillas from one of his favorite Mexican restaurants.

"Oh, man. You didn't have to do that. How kind of you."

Mike approached Clara, but the phone rang.

"Sorry, I'm expecting an important call. Hold that thought for one second." He gestured.

While she waited for Mike, thoughts began to reel in her mind about this convenient little arrangement he had with Savannah working at the front desk.

Why hadn't he mentioned it to me? This is the typical crap that guys do when they want to have their cake and eat it, too. I feel like such an idiot. Her eyebrows were lowered and drawn together as Mike hung up the phone.

"You look upset. Is everything okay?" he asked

"I don't know, Mike. You tell me. I actually just stopped by to bring you lunch and check out the new place. You can only imagine how surprised I was to run into Savannah. What's the matter? You forget to mention that she's one of your new hires?"

"Clara, I can explain. She's not a new hire. She's only working here temporarily until she can get back on her feet."

"Of all the places for her to get back on her feet, she had to come to you? Give me a break, Mike. To think, you gave me such a hard time when Keith showed up. This is so much worse," she said.

"Why? There's nothing going on between us. I swear. Her father sent a few connections my way when I was doing the research to find this place. In return, he asked for a favor to help with a temp position until she gets back on her feet. She's searching for a job in a completely different field, Clara."

"That's not the point and you know it. The last thing you said to me was she was a thing of the past. Today, I walk in here and she's very much a thing of the present."

"I can see where you're coming from, but I promise there's nothing to it. Clara, believe me."

"No, Mike. I don't have to believe anything. If you really wanted to go about this the right way, you should've told me." She argued.

"Clara."

"It's okay, really. Look, I should get back to Solomons. Tommy is covering the front desk for me and I need to get back to relieve him," she said.

"Clara, don't do this. Let's be rational. Take a moment to talk this out with me. I don't want you leaving here upset."

Memories of every lie she'd ever been told by a man caused heat to rise from within. She flopped his lunch bag and his drink down on the desk, sending the drink toppling into Mike's lap.

Feeling awkward and frustrated, she marched right out of the room, leaving him there to clean up the mess on his own.

Back in the car, Clara sped down route four, infuriated and pressing the ignore button every time Mike rang her phone.

This is exactly why you don't date your boss, Clara. Bad idea. It's all roses when you're getting along. But when he cheats and treats you like you don't have enough sense to figure it out, then what?

She stared at the red light in front of her, nervously tapping on the steering wheel.

Then there's Savannah. The nerve of her sitting there practically gloating when she saw my face. Ugh!

The rest of the ride was spent in silence, replaying the scene in her head over and over again.

~

That evening Clara sat in a booth alone at the café. Mackenzie was off for the night and with Chloe and Joshua serving, she knew she could be alone with nobody really noticing. She picked at her meal and stared at the baseball game on the big screen. She even listened as the bridge club argued over their game. Basically, she did anything she could to keep her mind off Mike and Savannah.

"Are you hiding from me now?" Mike asked.

Clara jumped, startled to hear his voice at first, followed by feelings of being irritated.

"No."

"Then how come you're not taking any of my calls?" he asked.

"There's nothing to talk about. Whoever you choose to work for you is your business, not mine."

He took the seat across from her, reaching his hand out, but she withdrew.

"Clara, I had to walk out of the store, looking like I wet my pants, all because you think I'm sleeping with Savannah... which couldn't be further from the truth, by the way."

"I didn't say a thing about you sleeping with her. I took note that you intentionally avoided telling me she's working for you. Whether it be temporary or not, don't you see that as a conflict of interest? Hello, she's the woman you last dated before we started seeing each other, Mike. At least when Keith showed up, I didn't lie to you about who he was and what he was doing. What's your excuse? Now that I think of it, she stopped by the Solomons office the week Keith was in town. I guess you two never really stopped being an item after all," she said.

"That's not true. Stopping by that time was her own doing. Whereas now, the temp job is a favor that her father asked for. Two very different situations."

"There was no part of you that thought this would be a bad idea? You could've told the guy that you'd keep your eye out for a position in Solomons. Every time we're around each other all she does is say something that alludes to you two being together," Clara responded.

"I'm sorry, I didn't realize she did that."

"That's because she behaves like a perfect angel when you're around. Again, I don't want to influence you one way or the other. I just don't want to have anything to do with her. From now on I'll stay put, right here on Solomons Island. This whole thing was probably a bad idea, anyway."

She sat as far back as she could, twirling her fork around in her food, wishing she had gone straight home.

"I disagree with you. You're not going to like what I have to say, but you need to hear it. I think you're afraid... afraid to get burned by another man. Sure, now that you mention it, I could've chosen a different way to handle the Savannah situation, but Clara, she's literally there for two more weeks, and I barely have enough time to speak to her as it is. I'll ask her to cool it, and I'll even do it with you present if that will make things better. But, you need to know, I'm not that guy. I don't date multiple women at the same time, and I'm not a liar. I've never been that guy, and I'm not going to start now. Even if you don't believe me," he said.

She searched his eyes for the slightest ounce of dishonestly but found nothing.

"I believe you, but I'd definitely prefer you being

more upfront with me next time. I don't think that's asking too much," she replied.

"Agreed."

Clara picked up her fork again, attempting to eat something before the entire plate grew cold.

∾

After leaving the café, Mike asked her to join him for an evening stroll along the dock across the street. He hopped over the fence leading down to the beach and extended his hand toward Clara.

"Are you crazy?" she said, looking around to see if anyone was in sight.

"Crazy about you. Come on, people take this shortcut all the time." He begged.

"My mother used to ask me if someone jumped off a bridge, would you follow them?"

"She sounds like a wise woman. Except this is an innocent little jump that will lead to something good. Trust me."

She looked over her shoulder once more and then hopped the fence, landing against Mike's chest.

"This better be real good, Sanders. You see that sign... no trespassing allowed. If I get arrested-" She complained.

"You won't get arrested, and we won't stay that long. I just want to show you something."

He led her by the hand past the dock and the

back entrance of his business to a rocky area. She could see nothing but sand and rocks for miles, and she noticed Mike searching for something in particular.

"There it is, over there." He continued leading her to one of the larger rocks on the beach and made a comfortable place to sit, patting the rock firmly for her to join him.

"Come. Dream with me for a few minutes."

"Dream with you?" she asked.

"Yes. No one knows this about me, but this is where I come when I need to get away, clear my head, and even make plans for my future. Similar to the way you have your special place at the beach house, I have mine," he said while repositioning himself on the rock.

"This rock is where all my future planning began for opening up the new store."

"I love it. I think it's great to have a place to call your own. A place to clear your mind, dream, and make future plans." She drew her knees up to her chest and inhaled the smell of the water.

"This is also the place where I often came when I wanted to connect with my fiancé, Jenna."

Clara's face grew somber.

"It sounds crazy, I know. After all these years, you'd think I wouldn't do that, anymore. She's been gone for quite a while now. But I always made this little pact that I'd get still every once in a while and do all the things necessary to... I don't know... help keep her memory alive. I figured it was okay to do, at least until I met the right one to share this spot with."

"I think that's beautiful, Mike. I'm sure she's present in spirit, watching over you."

"The thing is... I know Jenna would tell me it's time to let go. She'd tell me it's time to move forward and work on fulfilling new dreams." Mike glanced over at Clara and held her hand.

"I brought you here to share my intentions with you, Clara. I see a bright future ahead of me, and it includes you in it... by my side. That's if you want to be, of course. I promise you, with everything in me, I only have eyes for you. Not Savannah, or anyone else. Just you."

"Wow. I didn't see that coming. Who would've thought this afternoon's lunch surprise would turn into all this?" she said.

"Hopefully, I'm not scaring you away."

"You're not. It would take a lot more for you to scare me away. While that move you pulled with not telling me about Savannah was rather stupid, deep down I know you're a good guy. I'm going to hold you to your promise." She smiled.

"That's fine by me. I like accountability, especially coming from you."

He pulled her gently in front of him, wrapping his arms around her waist from behind as they watched the tranquil water. It was a summer evening to be remembered. Clara kept her eyes closed and enjoyed his touch before she was reminded of her current reality.

"Mike."

"Yes."

"Since we met, it's been one thing after the other. First Joan's family, then my ex. I'm currently in the middle of filing for a divorce for goodness' sake. Doesn't that bother you at all?"

"Absolutely not. It would bother me if you weren't going through with the divorce. Then you could never really be mine, but that's not the case. As for Joan's family, I was happy to be there for you. I wanted you to feel safe."

He turned her around and kissed her. First slowly, then passionately. She released all her concerns, allowing them to dissipate with the touch of his lips and his firm hands caressing her.

Toward the end of their kiss, he brushed her hair to the side. "Maybe I'm not one of the good guys after all."

"What do you mean?"

"Well, technically, I just kissed a married woman." He teased.

Clara swatted at him and threatened to deliver another sweet tea to his desk if he didn't take it back.

CHAPTER 15

"I'm not impressed by your hot shot lawyer, his fancy letterhead, or these divorce papers, Clara." Keith snarled on the other end of the telephone line.

"Have you lost your mind? Calling me like this and making a spectacle of yourself? I don't care if you're impressed. The only thing I care about is you signing the papers so we can be done with this already. Isn't that what you wanted when you came here to Maryland in the first place? Now, you're about to get your wish," she said.

"That's not what I asked for and you know it. You still haven't delivered what I asked of you, but I know how to get you back. These papers... I'm not signing them." In the background, Clara could hear Keith ripping the papers repeatedly.

"I think you're getting great pleasure out of making me miserable, Keith. Just like you did when we were married. You haven't changed one bit. You are still the lowest scum of the earth." She cried angry tears but didn't reveal it in her voice.

"Bricks and stones may break my bones, but your words don't phase me." He snarled.

"That's not how the saying goes, you idiot."

"It's close enough. So, now that I tore up the papers, what are you going to do about it? You going to run and tell your hot shot lawyer?" he asked.

"Actually, you're making this rather easy for me. According to the law, you have thirty days to respond, and if you don't, you're just making it easier for the judge to rule in my favor. So, keep it up. Have at it. Throw your little temper-tantrum, I don't care."

"We'll see who gets to have the last word. This isn't over with. I deserve better treatment than this. The way you walked out on me wasn't right, and you should be held accountable for it," he replied.

"Give me a break, Keith. If you cared so much about how I left, then why did you wait all these years to act on it? Whatever, I don't even care to have this discussion with you. It's not worth my time," she said.

"It's interesting how-"

But before he could finish, she said, "Goodbye, Keith." She slammed the phone and disconnected the plug from the wall, crippling him from taunting her any further.

She spent several moments pacing barefoot around the back porch, inhaling and exhaling, trying to calm down. She contemplated whether calling Kolton and asking him to press charges was a good idea. *Press charges for what? What did he do exactly, besides tick me off?* She then considered taking other measures but settled with staying the course. *It's just thirty days... hang in there,* she thought.

She let Holly out and grabbed her cell out of the kitchen. This wasn't exactly the way she wanted to start her day off from work, but talking to her best friend might help ease things, so she dialed her number.

"Oh, no. What is it now? You have that recognizable sound in your voice," Mack said.

"I can't catch a break, Mack. I don't know what it is. I just want to be happy, that's all. Get up, go to work, enjoy Mike, Holly, the house... that's it."

"What happened?" she asked.

"Keith called first thing this morning. He received the divorce papers. It probably freaked him out because things aren't going according to his manipulative plan."

"He's calling you now?" she asked.

"He called the house. I'm sure it wasn't difficult for him to find the number online, it's public information."

"You know, Clara, when I was growing up, if anyone bothered me, my brother would pay them a visit and make them think twice about bothering me again. He only had to do it a few times. After that, everyone received the message loud and clear. That's what Keith needs... somebody to pay him a special visit."

"I hear you, but we're not young kids anymore, and there's a designated place for people who do things like that. It's called jail. I'd rather avoid that place at all costs." Clara laughed.

"Well, at least I made you smile. You need something to help you lighten up. I promise it may not feel like it now, but there's a light at the end of the tunnel."

"I know. Life has just done a complete one-hundred-eighty degree spin on me. Literally last year this time, I was an introverted housekeeper who spent most of her days at the house, the beach, or the café. Life may have been a little boring, but it was peaceful." She explained.

"Okay, so you added one more location to the list of travels, Lighthouse Tours. I don't care what you say, you're still an introvert. You just peeked your head out of your shell at the right time to meet a good man and get a good job." Mack chuckled.

Clara nodded while watching Holly kick up dirt and sand in the back.

"This all boils down to one thing. Make up your

mind that you're determined not to let this defeat you. After that, press forward and move on. If not, the only way I know how to get back to your old way of life is to tell Mike it was nice dating him for a little while, but no thanks. Then, sell the house, give all your money away, apply for a housekeeping job else-where, and try your best to mirror what once was. Is that what you really want?"

"No."

"I didn't think so. If that jerk of an ex-husband calls or shows up one more time, I'll deal with him personally. I learned a thing or two from my brother and I earned a black belt in karate," Mack said.

"You are such a nut, but I love you for it. Thanks for cheering me up."

"Anytime. That's what friends are for. Now, when are we getting together again? I could use a pick-me up. Bill's out of town this weekend and Stephanie is at camp. I almost considered going into the café before you called."

"You should come over. Maybe we can take a drive up to Chesapeake Beach just to get out for a while," Clara said.

"We could, but you have a beach right there in your backyard. I'll take the privacy over the crowded beach any day of the week."

"Sounds good to me."

"I'll bring lunch for the two of us." Mack offered.

"Perfect. I actually could use a few ideas for

something else. Have you seen Jonathan or Ms. Mae lately?"

"No. They normally stop in every once in a while, but I haven't seen either of them."

"I'm not shocked. They've been going through a bit of a rough patch. Here's the thing. I'll go into more detail when you get here, but I may need your help in coming up with a plan to get them to the house. Ms. Mae needs another opportunity to... finish what Jonathan started." Clara's voice trailed off, not feeling certain about how much to reveal.

"I'm not sure I'm following you," Mack said, sounding curious.

"Let's just put it this way. Those two are supposed to be engaged by now, but things didn't exactly go according to plan. We're going to see what we can do to create the right atmosphere where they can hopefully get back on track," she replied.

"Got it. So, I'll bring the sandwiches, drinks, and all the right fixings for helping two people get hitched. See you around noon."

"Ha! Perfect. See you then."

Mike admired the old rustic sign for Chesapeake Charters in the front of his new business. There was a sense of pride he felt in finally owning something that was one hundred percent his. *This one will be*

different from the Solomons business, he thought. He pulled his jeep into the space out front, put the gear in park and glanced at the sign once more before heading inside.

Savannah greeted him with her usual overzealous and flirtatious personality, which he usually ignored. This time he was sensitive to it, given his conversation with Clara.

"Good morning, Savannah. Have you seen Brody by any chance? I need to run a few things by him," he asked.

"No, I'm not sure that he's coming here today. I think he mentioned something about spending his day in Solomons Island so he could work on a few boat repairs."

"Hmm, that's interesting. Maybe I missed something on the schedule. No problem. I'll be in the back if you need me." He walked away, completely overlooking the tight dress she was wearing as she stood up.

"Mike, can we chat for a few minutes? There's something I was hoping to discuss before your day picks up," she said.

"If it's not an emergency, I really have a ton of things I need to get to before the first tour heads out today. I was actually going to ask you to hold all my calls for at least the next hour."

"It won't take long. I promise. I just needed to go over plans for my last day and perhaps talk about taking time off to go on a few more interviews. I promise I'll be really quick," she replied.

"Interviews. Wow, that's great. Yeah, sure, we can talk briefly. I actually need to put plans in place for hiring someone." He felt a weight lifted off his shoulder. Perhaps this would be easier than he thought. With Savannah gone, he hoped this would put Clara's mind at ease.

"It will take five minutes, tops," she said.

"Okay, let me just put my bags down in my office and I'll be right back."

Mike walked to the back and dropped his bags by the door. He opened the blinds, letting the sunlight in, and turned to see Savannah making herself comfortable in one of his chairs.

"Well, this must be very important. You seem eager to talk," he said.

"It is important."

He noticed the door was closed, but again, he chalked it up to being overly sensitive and maybe extra cautious, which wasn't a bad thing.

"I just wanted to update you on how things are going with the job interviews," she said.

"Any prospects?"

"Not quite," she responded.

"What happened? I thought you had at least two promising opportunities. Did you hear from them yet?"

"I did. The first company, which would've been

my dream job, went with someone else. The second company is still conducting multiple rounds of interviews with several candidates before making their final decision. I've been on pins and needles waiting to hear, but the reality is this entire process may take longer than expected. Since you haven't hired anyone yet..." She hinted.

"I was hoping..."

He knew what she was about to say and felt a sense of awkwardness between them.

"Savannah."

"Wait, hear me out. I was hoping I could stay a little while longer." She inched toward the edge of her seat, revealing her cleavage and the full length of the side slit in her dress.

"Mike, I could really use your help. I'll even work overtime if you need me to. You know I'd do anything for you," she said.

"I appreciate it, but what I really need most is to train the new hire so they can learn the job and get to know the lay of the land. I can't pay you both, Savannah. I just don't have it in my budget," he said.

"I know, but what if we work something out where we split the shift at first? This way, they can slowly transition into learning the job, and I still have a little income to hold me over while I continue to interview?"

He closed his eyes, shaking his head no.

"Sorry, but I don't think it's a good idea. Time is

of the essence when it comes to running a new business, and I just can't see how this plan would be beneficial," he replied.

She sulked and softened her voice a bit.

"You used to have a soft spot for me, Mike. You used to drop everything on a dime to be there for me. What happened?" she asked.

"The fact that you've been here this long is a good show of support, don't you think? When your dad called in the favor, I responded without hesitation. But, you always knew this was temporary, just to help get things up and running while you continued your job search."

Savannah walked over to the bookshelf located slightly behind his desk. She picked up a picture of him standing in uniform with a group of guys from his time of service in the coastguard and smiled.

"This is such a handsome photo of you. It kind of reminds me of how you looked when we met. You were still wearing those military buzz cuts back then." She laughed.

He leaned back in his swivel chair and listened.

"Do you remember those days? You just moved from Annapolis. The Solomons store hadn't been open for a week before you came strolling into the café, asking for Chef Harold to give you the best thing they had on the menu."

He laughed.

"You remember that?" he asked.

"I sure do. How could I forget? You stood out in the crowd. I hadn't seen a man that good looking in Solomons in a long time. Besides the good looks, I knew there was something special about you. There's always been something special about you, Mike."

He sat upright in his chair and cleared his throat, recognizing her art of seduction and not willing to fall prey.

"Savannah, a lot has changed since then. I've moved on and I have no intentions of revisiting the past. We've gone over this already. This temp position was purely offered as a favor and nothing more."

She put the picture back down and made her way closer to his door.

"Interesting, you didn't seem to mind revisiting your past before Clara showed up. Now, it's like I don't even exist," she said in a snarky tone.

"That's not true and you know it. We stopped seeing each other beforehand. Not that I have to justify my actions to you or anyone else. Savannah, you're really out of line here. I'm doing you a favor... one that's causing more friction than I care to deal with."

"I'm doing the best that I can. What do you want from me, Mike?"

She dabbed her eyelids and sniffled. Mike wondered if she was on the verge of having a miniature meltdown or if it was another one of her award-winning performances.

"It's fine... I'll figure something out. I've dealt with much worse so it's not the end of the world," she said.

He fiddled with the pens in a nearby jar before addressing her comment.

"Look, I'm not going to just kick you out of here, but I need to focus on starting interviews in the next thirty days. If I were you, I would go hard on the interviews and if that doesn't work out, put a back-up plan in place to apply at a temp agency until you find the ideal job."

"Thank you, Mike. Thank you so much, you won't regret it." She stepped forward to hug him but thought better of it.

"There's one more thing. It's important that we maintain a professional atmosphere around here at all times. That includes the way you interact with me... are we clear?"

She rolled her eyes.

"Anything else?"

"Savannah."

"All right, all right. A strictly professional environment from here on out. Gee, somebody woke up on the wrong side of the bed this morning." She sighed.

He motioned for her to close the door. When she did, he massaged his head, wondering why he was stupid enough to get himself in this predicament in the first place.

CHAPTER 16

$\mathcal{M}$ ae arrived at Clara's house, instantly identifying Jonathan's truck and not feeling too pleased about it. Days had passed since they last saw each other, and the last thing she wanted was another uncomfortable encounter.

I could've sworn I told her I'd think about it, she thought. Before she could think of an excuse to leave, she saw Clara waving from the front door.

Mae rolled the window down.

"Clara, I don't know what you're up to, but I have to go," she said.

"Mae, you can't leave. Jonathan is out back looking at the boat," she whispered.

"And? I can think of plenty of things to do on a Sunday morning besides trying to talk to someone who has no interest in hearing what I have to say. You should've been upfront with me," she said while remaining in the car.

Clara peeked over her shoulder and then walked to Mae's window.

"Let's be rational about this, Ms. Mae, please. I know I could've come right out and told you why I was inviting you over instead of making up some silly excuse, and I apologize for that. But, here's the thing. He's right out back tinkering around with the motor as we speak. I can't imagine you'd want to miss an opportunity to talk knowing he's this close," she said.

"Well, imagine it. I thought long and hard about this. Jonathan doesn't care to hear what I have to say, anymore. He walked out on me. I'm not sure why that's so difficult for you to understand," she said, sounding discouraged.

Clara threw her hands up in frustration.

"Sometimes I wonder why I'm so invested in helping you two. This doesn't make any sense. You both have a lot in common, you know. You're stubborn, you have all the answers, you won't ever let anybody help you, and you both walk around drowning in your own misery. Did I mention that you're stubborn?" Clara asked.

"Twice."

"Good! You probably needed to hear it twice. Now, if you won't do it for yourself, can you please....please... get out of this car and go talk to the man for me? Life has been one heck of a roller coaster ride these past several months, and it's about time we turn things around and start experiencing something good. Wouldn't you agree?"

Mae's hands rested on the steering wheel while looking straight forward toward the house.

"Mmm." She groaned.

"Ugh, this is crazy. Do something. I don't know how much longer the staff can stand watching you two, walking around, ignoring each other the way you do. If you won't do it for me, think about everyone else." Clara begged.

"They don't care. Tommy's busy, and Brody has been spending a lot of time with Mike."

"So, you're just going to give up? Just like that?" she said.

Jonathan's voice startled the women. "What's she doing here?"

He had a wrench in hand and wore his favorite overalls for whenever he planned on getting dirty. The wrinkles in his furrowed brows remained as he tried to figure out why Mae was sitting in the car.

"Go ahead, Clara. Explain to Jonathan why I'm here in your driveway when I could be home tending to my flower garden."

Clara looked Jonathan in the eyes and then glanced over at Mae again.

"I'm here because Clara thought it was a good idea to play matchmaker. You think you're here to fix the boat, but she really wanted to create an opportunity for us to talk."

"Is that so?" he asked Clara.

"Well, mostly, yes, but the boat does need a little tlc. Please don't be mad. I really had the best intentions. Things were stuffy between you two at work and I thought..."

"You shouldn't have," he said.

Mae gave him a look. She wasn't thrilled about being there, but now she wanted him to explain himself. Although annoying, it was still a kind gesture from Clara, done in the name of saving their relationship.

"Why shouldn't she?" Mae asked.

Clara and Jonathan both looked surprised at her question.

"You weren't exactly willing to hear anything I had to say, Jonathan."

"I listened to you. But, I still wasn't convinced that anything changed," he said.

"I don't understand. I poured out my heart to you, and you walked right out the door as if everything I said meant nothing to you."

"That's your perspective. From where I sit, a person's actions speak louder than their words." He walked over to the back of his truck and started sifting through his toolbox. She noticed Clara backing away but got out of the car and followed behind Jonathan.

"Well, what are my actions telling you then?"

"Oh, Mae, I'm not doing this now," he responded.

"Why not? Tell me. I want to know."

He looked at her.

"Your actions say you care about me, but not enough to spend the rest of your life with me. You were saying all the right things that day, but if your heart's not in it, what does it matter? Being with you is a choice I intentionally make every single day. You play by another set of rules. Sometimes you want to be with me and other times I think you'd be perfectly happy being by yourself."

Mae stood on the opposite side of the truck and drew in a breath.

"I'm sorry you feel that way, Jonathan."

"That's it?" He called out.

"Yes, if my word isn't good enough, then I don't know what else I can offer you."

"How about offering a genuine desire to be with me? That's all I've ever wanted. I'll never be able to fulfill the role of your first husband, I get it. But, that doesn't mean I wouldn't die trying to make you the happiest woman alive." He closed the lid to his toolbox and waited for Mae to respond.

"Ask me again," she said.

"What?"

"Ask me again... Ask me to marry you. I promise you won't be disappointed at the outcome. This whole thing has helped me to realize I'm more afraid of losing you than anything else. My entire world would fall apart without you, Jonathan. Please, ask me again." Her voice was rattled, but she knew it was now or never.

"Mae, my heart is nothing to experiment with," he said.

"I wouldn't dare do such a thing. I'm very serious, Jonathan Middleton. Ask me."

"I don't have the ring, and we're standing in the middle of Clara's driveway for crying out loud," he replied.

"There's a beach out back and I don't need a ring to be happy. All I need is you. I'll propose, if that's what it takes."

"You would?" He slowly made his way around to her.

"Well, it's never been my first choice. I'm more traditional, but if that's what it takes to get through to you, I'll get down on my bad knee just to prove my love."

Jonathan chuckled.

"There she is... that sounds more like the Mae I know."

"So, what do you say? Will you give it one more try?" she asked.

"I'll do one better, Mae. If you're really sincere about spending the rest of your life with me, then let's toss all the formalities to the side. Let's drive to the courthouse and get married in the morning... that way we can move on with our lives and put this thing behind us once and for all."

"Tomorrow? Wow, I guess we could. But, what about giving the family time to drive down and be with us for a small ceremony? Wouldn't you want them to be present?" she asked.

"We can always have a reception here on the island with our closest friends and family. We can arrange all that later in the summer, or perhaps the fall. The only thing I care about is having you as my wife. How we go about it is secondary to me."

Mae was quiet for a moment and then planted both hands on his cheeks.

"Jonathan, I think it's a wonderful idea. There's no sense in putting this off any longer. I'm going to pick out one of my best dresses, fix up my hair for you, and tomorrow, we're going to get married." She kissed his lips, feeling elated to be back in his arms again.

"So, does this mean I get to smell your burned toast in the mornings, for the rest of our lives?" she asked.

"Yep, unless you want to make breakfast. Sorry, it comes along with being a Middleton." He laughed.

"Mae, I missed you so much," he said. Then, he looked up, noticing a not-so-innocent bystander watching from the front door.

"Looks like we have company. Do you think we should break the news to her?" he asked.

Mae motioned for Clara to come over.

"She did play a role in bringing us back together. Plus, she's the one who has to figure out who's going to cover our shifts while we're off getting hitched," she said.

"That's all right, a few of the guys over at the marina would be happy to make some extra change for the day."

By noon on Monday, Clara lined up a couple of college students to fill in for Jonathan and Mae's shifts. Occasionally, when Mike needed some extra hands on deck, the owner of the local marina would send some of his seasonal college students to lend a helping hand. It was the only place to find help on such short notice. She often wondered why he didn't consider expanding the staff with a few part-timers. He mentioned it one time, but the Lighthouse company was more of a small mom and pop operation, and it seemed like he preferred keeping it that way.

"Mike, meet David and Shelton. They're taking over the tours for this afternoon," she said.

"David... Shelton... nice to have you fellas. Thanks for coming through for us on such short notice," Mike said, shaking their hands.

"No problem, sir. We're here for the summer, so

if you need help with anything, you can always call us," Shelton replied.

"I appreciate it. Clara mentioned you guys are experts with handling the boats and you actually handle similar tours down at the marina, correct?"

"Yes, we do. I'd love to check out the fishing equipment, just to make sure I know how everything is set up. I'm more of the fishing expert. Shelton can cover the island tour with his eyes closed," David said.

"Perfect. Right this way, gentlemen."

Clara watched them head out back and then returned to review the schedule for the rest of the week. She thought it might be nice to call and offer Mae and Jonathan a couple of days off, but she'd leave that up to Mike to decide. Tommy was expected to arrive in another hour, which allowed plenty of time to bring Mike up to speed on everything.

"Thank you for calling Lighthouse Tours. How may I help you?" she said, answering the telephone.

"Good morning, my fiancé and I are visiting family in Solomons Island for the week. We drove by yesterday and noticed your sign for Lighthouse Tours. I was wondering if you offer private tours for two? I'd love to plan a romantic surprise for us to enjoy during our stay."

"Sure. We can set up a tour for Thursday afternoon if you'd like." She offered.

"Thursday would be great."

She entered his information into the system and confirmed a time for Thursday afternoon.

"All right, I think we're all set. I look forward to meeting you and your fiancé. Take care." She hung up and watched Mike bring in a UPS delivery on a dolly.

"Love is definitely in the air this week." Clara smiled.

"Why? Because of Jonathan and Ms. Mae? Those two have been in love since they started working for me in Annapolis. I'm surprised they waited this long to tie the knot."

"Well, apparently they're not the only ones in love. A guy just booked a private tour for him and his fiancé this week. It's a surprise, and he sounded so happy to arrange it for her. It was so sweet."

He stopped what he was doing and gave her a peck on the cheek.

"She's not the only one in for a surprise this week," he said.

"Really? What are you planning?"

"If I told you, it wouldn't be a surprise. Just be sure to meet me at my place on Friday evening around nine." He smiled.

"Nine? I'm usually in my pj's by then."

"I can't leave the job any earlier than that, but you can come in your pj's if you want." Mike teased.

"Ha ha, very funny. I bet you'd get a kick out of

that, wouldn't you?"

"I wouldn't be upset by it, but that's beside the point. Just make sure you're there by nine. I've never led you astray with my surprises in the past and I don't think you'll be disappointed this time. In the meantime, you and I need to go over a few things. This week I plan to start my new schedule of working Monday and Wednesdays at this location and the other days in North Beach. Is there anything pressing that I need to know before I bury my head in the mail and start making phone calls?"

"Yes. The lights have been flickering in the break room. I'm not sure if something is going on with the electrical or what, but you need to have it checked out. I'd be happy to call an electrician if you want me to. Also, I know you're focused on North Beach right now, but things have been ramping up. I could easily book more tours and help increase revenue if we had additional hands on deck," she said.

"We just added Tommy."

"And he's working out great as your replacement. But, I promise you, if we had two part-timers, and perhaps even another full-time staff member, we could really turn things up a notch." Clara tried to make a case for why it might be a good idea, knowing that Mike might not agree.

"Now I see why you spent so much time dreaming of owning your own business. You really do have an entrepreneur's spirit. That's going to come in real handy around here. Of course, I don't have the final say on these kinds of decisions. I have to run it by my business partner, and I'm not sure he's going to be thrilled to hear ideas about expanding, given that I'm dividing my time between the two businesses. He'll think it's a direct result of me splitting my time," he said.

"Yeah, I didn't think about it like that."

"Not to worry. I like the way you think. It's attractive. Everything about you is attractive." He tugged on one of her curls.

"Mike, are you flirting with me on the job?" She started blushing.

"I might be. It depends on how receptive you are to it. There's no way I can sit here all day, looking at you, without wanting you, Clara. It's impossible."

He kissed her neck and breathed in the scent of her hair. It drove her crazy, sending chills all over her body. He kissed her again. She found every moment of it to be pleasurable, until she opened her eyes to see Shelton standing by the door.

"Eh em, Mike," she whispered. "I think Shelton needs you." She pointed behind him.

"Shelton, buddy. How can I help you?" he asked.

Clara giggled and returned to her computer. *I'll bet that will teach him a lesson,* she thought. Although, if she was being honest with herself, she loved it, and wanted to experience more of him with each passing day.

205

CHAPTER 17

$\mathcal{C}$lara sat in the lotus potion, practicing what she learned from her yoga videos on the dock. With the warmth of the late June sun rising above her and nothing but the peaceful sound of the shore, she could sit there for hours, meditating, and losing herself in the silence. Unfortunately, the ringing of her phone put a quick end to her peaceful bliss.

"Hello."

"Clara, it's Kolton. Sorry to bother you so early. I thought I'd try and catch you before you head out to work."

"Hi, Kolton. No worries, you know I always look forward to hearing from you. Do you have any updates for me?" she asked.

"I sure do. One that I think you'll be particularly happy to hear. The first update came in the form of a surprise call from your ex. He explained that he talked to you and after further consideration, he wasn't going to put up a fight. It looks like we can go after an uncontested divorce, which is the easiest route by far."

Clara unraveled her legs out of her yoga position, stunned by what she was hearing.

"Really? I wonder what changed his mind," she said.

"I thought surely you did. Either way, it's the outcome we're looking for so I won't complain."

"Interesting."

"There's more. It was so busy yesterday, I didn't have a chance to reach out to you. But, I did put in a call to one of my buddies who's a judge. Given the circumstances, it looks like he may be able to help us speed things along. If everything else goes well, it's very likely you'll be a free woman no later than mid-July. Early July is more like it, but I don't want to make any promises I can't keep."

She laughed and cried out all at the same time. Holly ran down the dock to be with her.

"Kolton, this is amazing. Are you serious?" she asked.

"I'm as serious as a heart attack. Okay, maybe that's a bad analogy, but you get the idea. You're going to officially be a single woman very soon."

"Oh, that sounds like music to my ears," she said.

"I figured it would. There's not much else to do

at this point but sit it out and wait to hear back from the court. I'll give you a call if anything new pops up."

"Thank you, thank you, thank you."

"You're more than welcome. Happy to deliver such good news," he responded.

"Good news, indeed."

On the way into work Clara stopped by the café. She ordered a danish and coffee but mainly stopped in to deliver the good news to Mackenzie.

"I've been meaning to call you this week. How did things work out with Ms. Mae and Jonathan?" Mackenzie asked.

"Well, let's just say all of our ideas went out the door the moment she arrived. Those two are as stubborn as bulls. One minute she's refusing to talk to him, the next they're having a spat in my driveway, and in the end, they wound up going to the courthouse on Monday, to officially become Mr. and Mrs. Middleton."

"What!" Mack shouted.

"Yep. As sure as what my name is, they're married and enjoying a three-day honeymoon."

"Oh my word. I didn't see that coming. Mae doesn't take me as the spontaneous type." Mackenzie laughed.

"I agree, but I think the idea of letting a good man slip away may have changed that."

"As long as they're happy, that's what matters most," Mack said.

"Speaking of happiness, you're glowing. Bill must be back in town. I've haven't seen you this happy in a long time."

"He is back. We've being seeing each other regularly since he returned. We even made arrangements for him to meet Stephanie this weekend," she replied.

"Oh, now that's an interesting turn of events. You must be getting pretty serious."

"Serious enough. Steph is starting to get curious about who I've been spending my time with. To be honest, I can't afford to keep getting a babysitter for all these date nights. Something has to give. Plus, I really want her to meet him. He's a good guy...a family man, which is something we've been missing in our lives. I'm still being protective of her, though. I told Bill if he did anything to break my baby's heart, he'd have to answer to me," Mack said while holding up her fists.

"I'm sure he doesn't want to do anything to get on your bad side."

"He better not, but enough about us. What's going on with you this week?" she asked.

"Let's see. Things are going pretty well with Mike. He's working out of the Solomons office a couple of days a week now."

"That's nice. I figured things were pretty good by the look of that grin on your face."

"Is it that obvious? Man, I better work on that. All kidding aside, he's planned a surprise for me on Friday night. I have no idea what it's about but I'm dying to know. If he stops by, see if you can pick his brain for me," Clara said.

"I'll do some investigating and see what I can find out."

"Thank you. The only other news I have to share is things are looking up with the divorce. Kolton called and told me he things he can get things expedited," she said.

"Oh, thank goodness. That would be amazing. The sooner you can get rid of that psychopath, the better."

"Gee, tell me how you really feel." She chuckled.

"I'm sorry, girl. I just think you could do without all the extra drama that comes along with still being married to him."

"That makes two of us. Mack, I'm really thankful for having you as a friend. You've been right by my side through it all, and I can't thank you enough," Clara said.

"We're friends so it comes along with the territory. No thanks needed. Now, what are we going to do about celebrating Jonathan and Ms. Mae's nuptials?"

"I'm don't know but count me out for now. I'm more than happy to help if they ask, but I've learned my lesson when it comes to poking my nose in other folks' business. I'm so thankful things worked out. If they hadn't, it's likely they wouldn't be speaking to me," Clara said.

"Nonsense. They love you too much. Plus, I would've confessed that I secretly played a role in the planning. Either way, I'm glad to see them get past their rough patch. That's what matters most."

"True." Clara placed her handbag over her shoulders and grabbed her danish.

"Taking off so soon?" Mack asked.

"Yes, we have a large group arriving this morning for the lighthouse tour. I want to make sure everything is in place before they arrive."

"All right, well say hello to the crew for me, and you tell Mike it's time for him to pay us a visit," she said.

"Will do."

Clara discovered a large arrangement of pink tulips waiting on her desk when she arrived. She inhaled the fresh scent of flowers and picked up a card with her name written on the front. *Thank you for being you. I couldn't keep things afloat at the store without you. Meeting you is the best thing that's ever hap-*

pened to me. Looking forward to our date Friday night. Love, Mike.

She looked over her shoulder, wondering if he decided to come in an extra day this week. She checked the back, only to find Tommy putting his things away in his locker.

"Hi, Tommy."

"Hey, Clara. I thought you were Mike for a minute. How's it going?"

"Everything is great. Did you see Mike this morning?"

"Yes, He stopped by to pick up a few things and then he was headed to North Beach," he said.

"Ahh, okay. Are you ready for this morning's tour? It's a big one. You have a party of twelve who will be excited to see every lighthouse this county has to offer," she said.

"Yes, ma'am. I was born ready. This has to be my fifth or sixth lighthouse tour, but I have to tell you, it never gets old to me. I think I discover something new every time."

"That's wonderful. I'm sure the experience will make you an even better tour guide. If only I could quit getting so nauseous out there on the water, I'd love to experience it again for myself," Clara responded.

"You suffer from sea sickness?" he asked.

"Yes, the worse kind. Mike seems to think it can

be conquered, but I don't think I have the mental will power."

"That's too bad. You're missing out."

"I'll have to take your word for it. If you need anything, I'll be up front clicking away at the computer."

Sounds good," he said.

She turned the corner and was taken back by Savannah standing at the front counter.

"Savannah, I didn't hear you come in."

"Yeah, I didn't exactly make an announcement or anything. I heard you talking in the back, so I figured I'd wait for you to come up front," she said.

Clara couldn't miss the awkwardness between them. That same awkwardness that exists when two women have an interest in the same man, with one having the upper hand over the other.

"Pretty flowers," she said.

"Thanks."

"Let me guess. Did Mike give them to you?" Savannah said, making the atmosphere even more uncomfortable.

"Savannah, how can I help you?" Clara asked.

"I don't need anything in particular. I'm actually on my way to an interview this morning. It's not far from here. I thought I would stop by to let you know, you don't have to worry about me getting in the way of things between you and Mike."

"Savannah-"

"Let me finish, Clara. He didn't ask me to say this. He doesn't even know I'm here. So if you bring this up with him, that's on you. It's no secret that my presence at the North Beach office is causing friction."

"I'm not sure what you mean."

"He already told me... so there's no use in pretending. I'll admit, I still have feelings for him. What woman wouldn't want to try and rekindle love with a guy like Mike? He's perfect in every way. But, things didn't work out with us, and he made it very clear the other day that it never will. I'm not sure what he sees in you, but whatever it is, he's really into you."

Clara wasn't sure if she should take that remark as a compliment or not, but she continued to listen.

"Believe me when I tell you, the only reason Mike gave me the temp job was because of my dad. They have a history. There's no way Mike would say no to him. But, that's as far as it goes. There's nothing between us and I'm confident there never will be. Hopefully within the next couple of weeks I'll hear back from one of my interviews so I can be on my way," Savannah said.

Clara recalled the times she came into the store flaunting herself and being rude. Whatever Mike said must've really hit home for her to humble herself to this degree.

"I appreciate you sharing. I hope everything works out with your job interviews," she said.

"Thanks." She withdrew from the counter, giving the place a final once over before leaving Clara with a parting word.

"He always said he'd never marry again. Not unless he met a woman who raised the bar even higher than his fiancé did. I have this funny feeling you've been able to raise the bar. Good luck to you."

Clara watched as she disappeared out of the store, leaving her speechless. She wasn't sure what to make of the visit, but she felt relieved knowing Savannah was moving on with her life.

CHAPTER 18

*C*lara pressed the doorbell while observing the inviting appearance of Mike's cottage. It was freshly painted blue with white trim and a white picket fence out front. He had a lightbulb that created the illusion of a flame and a hanging bench swing on the front porch.

"Ah, there she is," he said, standing on the other side of the threshold.

"Here I am. I decided not to show up in my pj's after all. I didn't want to scare you away." She smiled.

"I don't think it's possible for you to scare anybody away. You look stunning."

"Thank you."

"I hate to do this, but if you could just wait right here for one more minute. I'll be right back. I just have to check on something before I reveal the surprise to you," he said.

"Okay. You have me really curious what it is. This better not be some sort of prank."

"I wouldn't dare. Come on, have I failed you yet? Just wait here. I'll be right back," he said.

She stood on the other side of his door somewhat peeking into his front window but wasn't able to see much.

I wonder what he's up to, she thought.

There was an amber glow that flickered from behind the blinds, but she assumed it was another one of his flamed lightbulbs. He opened the door again.

"Okay, so here's the thing. I planned something really special for you, or at least I thought it would be special, but now that I pulled it together, I'm not so sure. I hope you like it, but if you don't-"

"Mike."

"Yes?"

"I'm sure whatever it is I'm going to love it. The mere fact that you went to so much effort for me means a lot," she said.

"Okay. After me." He sighed and directed her toward his living room.

Inside there was a path of off-white candles that trailed from his living room down a hallway. There were tall candles, short ones, there were so many she guessed he had to have spent at least an hour setting them up.

"Mike, this is beautiful," she said

"Thanks, but it's just a pathway leading to the surprise. Follow me."

He took her by the hand and led her to a door leading to his back porch.

"Before we go outside, you should know that my place doesn't come close to being as fancy as yours. I don't have a beach and we certainly can't go sailing off into the sunset, but I still hope you like it," he said, appearing to be a little nervous.

Outside, there were more candles covering the perimeter of his deck, and in the corner, a cellist played softly. Clara drew in both hands covering her mouth.

"Wow. This is absolutely amazing, Mike."

"It's all for you. I wanted to find a way to express my love for you. This is all I was able to come up with on a late Friday night after work. I hope you like it." He chuckled nervously.

"Like it? That's an understatement," she responded, wiping a tear from her eye.

"He's playing one of my favorite songs. It's called You Are the Reason. I chose it because you're the reason I feel alive again...you're the reason I'm ready to love again. I know we didn't meet under traditional circumstances, and you weren't always comfortable with us dating while working in Solomons together. Then, to make things worse, I made a poor choice to hire Savannah as my temp. But-"

She grabbed him and kissed him tenderly, not caring to hear explanations but desiring to savor every moment.

"Whew, you sure know how to make a man forget what he was saying." He smiled.

"And you know how to make a woman forget she was ever lonely. I almost forgot what it was like to have a good man in my life until I met you, Mike Sanders."

"Dance with me," he whispered.

The cellist picked up the tempo slightly, playing romantic hits and then salsa selections, setting the mood. The scent of Mike's body and the gentle swaying to the music served as a sweet seduction, causing her to want him even more. Her heart was palpitating, but she didn't allow her nervousness to show. *You're still technically a married woman, even if only for a few more days,* she thought.

"Not only are you spoiling me, but you're raising the bar pretty high for yourself, sir."

"I considered that, but if this is what a guy has to do to win your heart, then I'll do whatever it takes," he said.

"You already have my heart. In a matter of days, maybe a couple of weeks max, the divorce will be behind me, then we can do this thing right. You and me. Together."

"Really? Did you get an update from your lawyer?" he asked.

"Yes, I was going to share it with you tonight. He's friends with a judge who's going to help speed the process along."

"Yes! That's wonderful news." He picked her up and spun her around. They laughed together like teenagers in love.

"Mike, I have to tell you. I'm pretty impressed that you would go out of your way like this. It means a lot to me." She smiled.

"I'm glad you like it. I figured if you were still willing to put up with me after this week's fiasco, then it was the least I could do."

"About that. Savannah came to see me at the office this week," she said.

"Oh, no. What now?"

"Nothing, it's good actually. She was on the way to an interview nearby. She came to let me know that she was... how should I say it... moving on? She made it clear that she wouldn't be interfering, and she was focused on finding a new job and moving on with her life. It was almost like her version of an apology for her recent behavior."

"Savannah did this on her own?" He laughed.

"Well, yeah, I guess. I sure didn't invite her to stop by...did you?"

"No. I had a talk with her to set expectations and boundaries, but I never asked her to come by the office. I'm kind of glad she did. It's about time all that was put to rest. Now we can focus on our future to-gether. Just me and you," he said.

Clara laid her head on his shoulder as they con-tinued to sway to the music. In her eyes the evening couldn't be more perfect. She could've stayed and danced with him forever.

"Hey, Mike," she whispered.

"Yes?"

"I love you," Clara whispered.

Mondays always seemed to arrive quickly for Clara. She wasn't a morning person, but that only lasted as long as it took to hit the alarm and get out of bed. Af-terward, a splash of water on her face and a cup of coffee always made a difference.

This morning she was on her third round and feeling rather energetic when Jonathan and Mae arrived.

"Ladies and gentlemen. It is my pleasure to intro-duce to you Mr. and Mrs. Jonathan Middleton." Clara announced.

Brody, Mike, and Tommy whistled and cheered for them, making them both turn beet red. Even Mackenzie came across the street to be a part of the welcoming crew.

"Come here and give me a hug. I'm so happy for you guys," Mackenzie said.

"I can't stay long but I wanted to bring you a little gift." She continued.

"Oh, Mack. That's sweet of you, but you didn't have to buy us anything. We haven't even organized a reception yet." Mae pleaded with her.

"I bought it because I wanted to shower you with something special. As for a reception, I'm not sure what you have in mind. We plan on making sure you have a beautiful celebration with those who love you here at the job and the café. I'll bet the staff from the Annapolis office will want to come, too. Isn't that right, Mike?" Mackenzie said.

"It sure is. After we come up with the venue and the date, I'll call and coordinate with them. Congratulations, you guys. It warms my heart to finally see you two married. I'm just sorry I couldn't be there to witness it," Mike said.

Clara stood on the sidelines, watching everyone fuss over the bride and groom.

"Thank you, Mike. It was a spontaneous decision. But, one that we're happy with," Jonathan responded.

Tommy interjected.

"Ms. Mae...Mr. Jonathan...I haven't known you that long. But, one thing that became very obvious to me early on is you belong together. If I didn't know any better, I would've thought you were married already. All the best to you. Oh, and by the way, there have been so many requests for your fishing and island tours. I sure hope you're ready to dive back in because your clients can't seem to get enough of you," Tommy said.

"Tommy, thanks for the kind words and thank you for holding the fort down while we were gone. We really do appreciate it. To everyone, we just want to say thank you from the bottom of our hearts. Mike and Clara, we're so sorry for putting you in such a last-minute crunch with finding our replacements, but we thank you tremendously for extending our time to a full week. It meant the world to us." Mae added.

"I wouldn't have it any other way." Mike smiled.

Mack blew a kiss to Clara. "I have to head back. Call me later on so we can start making plans," she said.

Clara waved. Everyone talked for a few minutes before falling into their regular routine. Ms. Mae was the only one who lingered to play catch up with Clara.

"Do you have a few minutes to talk?" Mae asked.

"I always have time for you. What's on your mind?"

"I wanted to thank you personally, for putting yourself out there on a limb for me and Jonathan. If you hadn't arranged it so we could speak, this week may have never turned out the way it did," she said.

"You don't really mean that, do you? I would like to think eventually you would've gotten past this

223

little hurtle. Even though you both have strong wills, I think your love would supersede even the toughest disagreement, don't you think?"

"I'm sure you're right, but we both talked about it and agreed you played an important role. So, thank you, again," she said.

"Aww, you're welcome."

"I brought pictures to share from city hall." Mae laughed.

"It's nothing fancy, but we wanted to capture memories from the day, and we figured the family would enjoy seeing them. This one was taken with the staff that works behind the desk at the county clerk's office. What a nice bunch, I tell ya. They were kind enough to entertain me taking pictures of everybody. This picture is us standing with the justice of the peace. I swear the woman reminded me of Judge Judy. She looked just like her, except she was nice."

Clara chuckled. "Imagine that. A Judge Judy look-alike right here on Solomons Island!"

"I know, right!" They laughed together.

"Ohh, Clara. If I had one piece of advice for you pertaining to your future relationships, it would be to take whatever life dishes you and ride it like a bull. In other words, take control of the situation and don't let it take control of you."

"What makes you say that?" Clara asked.

"I almost let a good man slip away. I won't ever let fear grip me like that again. I had to learn to let go of my past and fully embrace what life was giving me in the present. Once I did, I felt free. Free as a bird. So, now I have a different take on things. Whatever life dishes out to me, I refuse to let it get the best of me. I'm going to ride it like a bull! At least that's what my folks used to say growing up, but I don't think I fully understood what it meant until now."

Clara twirled a strand of hair, considering if there were areas of her life where she too was allowing fear to have its grip on her life.

"It's something to think about, isn't it?" Mae said.

"It sure is. I'll have to keep that advice in mind."

"Good. How's everything going with you?" she asked.

"Great. The divorce is almost settled and here at the job I'm tackling marketing this week. I'm going to sit here and organize these fliers and maybe even head down to the boardwalk for a little inspiration this afternoon."

"What kind of inspiration are you looking for?"

"I was thinking, wouldn't it be nice to start building relationships with some of the businesses on the boardwalk? You never know. It might lead to a future connection or business opportunity. I'll bet people would love to stop and enjoy some of the seafood restaurants, the little chapels, boutiques, and some of the sights and sounds of Solomons Island," Clara said.

"I like the way you think. That's what I call job

security, so keep up the good work. Speaking of good work, I better get outside and crank up Blue Moon. Hopefully, the old gal still runs like a charm."

"You shouldn't have any problems with her. David and Shelton kept the boats warm for you guys, so you should be good to go."

Mae patted Clara on the shoulder.

"Thank you, darlin...not just for the boats, but for everything. I mean it."

"You're welcome. You and Jonathan are like family now. There isn't much I wouldn't do for you," she said.

"I knew you were one of a kind from the moment we met. Oh, and by the way, please tell Mackenzie she doesn't have to make a fuss over us. We plan on throwing something at a later date to celebrate."

"Listen, I wasn't going to poke my nose in it because I didn't want to get on your bad side, again. But, good luck telling Mackenzie or Mike not to throw you a party. Let me know how that turns out for you." Clara teased.

"Hmm. Well, if that's the case, make sure they keep it small. I'd hate for them to go all out and make a fuss," Mae yelled back and exited the room.

CHAPTER 19

"Shh, listen to that sound."

"What sound, exactly?" Mike asked.

"The sound of the waves crashing against the boats. It's so soothing," Clara replied.

"You know, for someone who gets seasick, I'm kind of surprised at your love for the water. I'm even more surprised that you agreed to a reception out here on the boat." He chuckled.

"Well, when Mack mentioned it to Mae, she lit up like the fourth of July. What was I going to do, disagree? Besides, we'll be docked the whole time, and I can't think of a more fitting theme for them. I mean, this is how it all began, right? She and Jonathan falling in love while sailing the ocean blue." She passed Mike ribbon to decorate with.

"The way you tell it sounds like such a fairytale."

"It is. Of course, with a few bumps along the road, but nevertheless, still a fairytale," she said.

Mike stopped to admire how beautiful she looked in her light-colored sundress.

"It's amazing to me how much you managed to change things around here in such a short period of time," he said.

"When I came here you already had something pretty special in place if you asked me."

"Yes, but it just feels better when you're around. Plus, you have all these wonderful ideas... a brand new way of looking at everything that I've never considered before. Remember the first time you ever helped me with tackling the books and tracking Brody's maintenance receipts?" he asked.

"Oh, boy. How could I forget? You had quite a disorganized system in place."

He flicked a little water at her from his water bottle.

"Hey, don't punish me for telling the truth." She teased.

"The sad part is you're right. My system was pathetic. But as always, you stepped right in and saved the day. I love that about you, Clara. It's like you complement me in every way. Not just here at the Lighthouse Company but in every single way."

Clara brushed her hand beside his cheek.

"Thank you. I take that as the ultimate compliment coming from you. However, you turned out to be a hero in your own right, you know."

"How's that?" he asked.

"My life was unraveling quickly when we met." She dusted off the cushions on the seated areas of the boat while continuing to talk.

"I wasn't prepared to change careers, I didn't have a plan, and my finances were looking pretty shabby at best. Then, it's like you showed up out of the clear blue sky and saved the day. I'll never be able to repay you for taking a chance on Clara, the housekeeper," she said.

"That's what happens when a beautiful woman backs into your car and accuses you of causing the accident. It makes you say and do crazy things." Mike laughed at his own sense of humor, but not for too long, wanting to stay on her good side.

"I'm teasing, I'm teasing. Look, on a serious note, have you given any thought to what I mentioned about you supporting me in more of an assistant manager role? I can really see us making a great team. You can oversee the day to day here and I'd still maintain my current schedule...nothing would change with that. I think we make a great team in more ways than one, Clara," he said.

"I've thought about it. I'm hoping it wouldn't require a ton of changes... at least not at first. If you agree, I'd still like to be the face that customers see when they come in and the voice they hear when they call to book appointments. I'm really enjoying that part of the job and I don't want to lose touch with it."

"Of course not. I think you should be the face of the Solomons Island office. I think the community would be disappointed if you weren't. I talked things over with my partner, Kenny. He's all for it. Then again, it really doesn't take much to impress him. As long as the numbers look good, he's happy. Honestly, since you've joined the team, the numbers have never looked better," he said.

"Well, if that's the case, then it's a done deal. I'm all yours."

"Do you mean it? Are you really all mine in every way imaginable?" He flirted.

It didn't matter if Mike was in her immediate presence or standing halfway on the other side of the boat. The attraction was strong, and she didn't mind letting it show.

"You are so naughty!" She giggled. "We only have two hours before everybody starts to arrive. Now, stay focused and help me finish these decorations."

"Yes, ma'am. As long as you stay on your side of the boat, we should be good." He smiled.

~

Mike made sure the calendar was clear that evening so everyone could celebrate Jonathan and Mae's union. His partner Kenny arrived with his wife and kids. Mackenzie brought Bill, her daughter Stephanie, and a few of their closest friends from the café. Mike tapped his glass with a spoon to get everyone's attention.

"Good evening, everyone. We're all gathered here tonight to celebrate two wonderful people who mean so much, not only to myself, the crew at the Lighthouse company, but to so many of us here in Solomons Island. I've told the story many times of how Ms. Mae and Jonathan came into my life in Annapolis. My partner Kenny and I wouldn't be where we are today without them. Isn't that right, Kenny?"

"You better believe it!" He whistled and raised his glass toward Jonathan and Mae.

"That's right. We feel honored to share this joyous occasion with you. A little birdie told me that at first Ms. Mae wouldn't hear of us throwing a party and making a fuss. But, quite honestly, I don't see how we couldn't. So, if everyone would raise their glasses, please. I'd like to make a toast. To Jonathan and Ms. Mae, the cornerstone of this company, we raise our glasses in celebration of your marriage this evening. May you live happy, healthy, and blissful lives together as husband and wife. We love you! Cheers!" Mike tapped his glass with the happy couple and took a celebratory sip.

Mack found Clara applauding in the crowd and snuck up next to her.

"When will I get to throw one of these soirees for you? Next year this time, maybe?" She mumbled so only Clara could hear.

"Oh, goodness. I knew it was only a matter of time before you'd start that again." Clara pretended to be annoyed by it but deep down she liked the idea a lot more than she let on.

"Can I at least become a single woman first? How about we revisit this topic after the whole process is complete?" she asked.

"That's progress. You used to resist the idea altogether. Now I see you're finally starting to come around. Fair enough. We can wait until then." She chuckled.

"Hush, let's listen. Jonathan is about to make a speech."

Jonathan approached the middle of the boat with Mae. He led her and tenderly kissed her hand before the crowd, then took the microphone to speak.

"In case you all haven't been able to notice, I am the happiest man alive, and I owe it all to this beautiful lady right here," he said, showing Mae off to the crowd.

"It's the best feeling in the world to know you have someone by your side who loves you unconditionally, through the good times, and the not so great moments. A couple of weeks ago Mae took the biggest leap of faith by joining me at the courthouse and becoming my wife. I plan on doing everything in my power to show her she made the right choice. To the Lighthouse staff, thank you for taking us in, giving us not only a job but a place to call home, and supporting us the way you do. For that, we are eternally grateful. Mae, would you like to add anything?" he asked.

"Sweetheart, I think you covered everything. Just know that we love you from the bottom of our hearts. To Mike and Clara, thank you. To Mackenzie, thank you for all this good food from the café. What a treat! And to Mike and Clara for creating a special venue for us, thank you. We're looking forward to an opportunity to celebrate you two... hopefully sooner than later."

Everyone clapped for Clara and Mike, not because they were shocked by the suggestion, but more so to cheer them on.

A few weeks after the celebration for the Middletons, things settled back to normal and Mike was finally figuring out how to balance his time between the two business locations. Savannah had moved on and accepted a position working as a secretary, and Clara was still learning her new role and loving every minute of it.

Most evenings what they enjoyed most were those quiet moments where they could settle in and enjoy each other's company. This particular evening, she set up her Adirondack chairs on the beach and relaxed with Mike, a glass of wine, and Holly by her side.

"How's things working out with the new assistant?" she asked.

"Pretty good, actually. So far Jan seems to be a pretty good fit. Her experience as a former 911 operator comes in handy. She's detail oriented, friendly, and doesn't take any nonsense when our seasonal workers act like they're relaxing on the job. She's a lot like Ms. Mae. She doesn't mind saying what's on her mind." He laughed.

"That's funny. You seem to have a knack for hiring someone to be the matriarch of the company. Perhaps she'll fit the bill."

"I didn't see it that way until now, but you have a good point there," he said.

Mike gently massaged the palm of her hand with his thumb while watching the full moon.

"Enough about me. How was your day?" he asked.

"Nothing short of amazing. All the tours went off without a hitch, and I received a call from the museum expressing an interest in doing business with you. They want to set up something in connection with your tours."

"Really? That's amazing. I'll give them a call tomorrow. Thanks, babe." He gave her a small peck on her temple.

"There's more. It's not business related but there's something I wanted to share with you. Something I received in the mail today." She passed him an envelope with the return address of the courthouse stamped at the top.

"Uhh, is this a good thing or..." He hesitated.

"Open it up and see for yourself," she said.

Mike pulled out the letter and reviewed its contents. A slow emerging smile appeared on his face as he read it. When he was done he got up out of his seat and extended his hand to Clara.

"Does this mean I get to start working on fulfilling my promise to you?" he asked.

With barely any space between them she said, "According to those papers in your hand, I'm a single lady now. So, I guess that means I'm completely available, if you want me."

"If? There's no question of whether or not I want you. I need you, Clara."

"Well, then, take me right here on this beach and fulfill every promise you've ever made to me. I need you just as much as you need me, Mike," she said.

They nestled to the ground and became lost in each other's tender embrace before settling in and holding each other under the moonlight. **Ready for book three of the Solomons Island series? Continue to learn more!**

Mike's ready to pop the question to Clara...

But, when news of a secret baby surfaces, will it ruin his plans for engagement?

Clara is happy in her relationship with Mike, but there's a major shift in focus when her sister shows up with bad news.

Solomons Island is a small and peaceful place, with lots of

love to go around. At the café, Clara's best friend, Mackenzie, is running the business as if it were her own, while balancing the busy life of a single mother. Her daughter is happy and so are her customers at work. If only she could translate that same level of happiness in her relationship with Bill. They've been dating for a while, but she's ready to take things to the next level. As they discuss their future, will she discover that Bill's heart is in a different place?

Mike's business, Lighthouse Tours, wouldn't be the same without Ms. Mae and Jonathan. These two prove that it's possible to work together and be married, and they do it very well. But at home, Jonathan and Mae still bump heads every now and again as they learn to merge households as Mr. and Mrs. Middleton.

There's nothing everyone wants more than a happily ever after. Join the characters of Solomons Island as they aim to fulfill their desire for love in the third book of the series, Beachfront Embrace.

Also By Michele:

Pelican Beach Series-

The Inn At Pelican Beach: Book 1

Sunsets At Pelican Beach: Book 2

A Pelican Beach Affair: Book 3

Christmas At Pelican Beach: Book 4

Sunrise At Pelican Beach: Book 5